SOME PLACES MORE THAN OTHERS

Books for older readers by Renée Watson

Watch Us Rise
(with Ellen Hagan)

Piecing Me Together
This Side of Home
What Momma Left Me

SOME PLACES MORE THAN OTHERS

Renée Watson

BLOOMSBURY
CHILDREN'S BOOKS
LONDON OXFORD NEW YORK NEW DELHI SYDNEY

BLOOMSBURY CHILDREN'S BOOKS
Bloomsbury Publishing Plc
50 Bedford Square, London WC1B 3DP, UK

BLOOMSBURY, BLOOMSBURY CHILDREN'S BOOKS and the Diana logo
are trademarks of Bloomsbury Publishing Plc

First published in the United States of America in 2019 by Bloomsbury Children's Books
First published in Great Britain in 2019 by Bloomsbury Publishing Plc

A catalogue record for this book is available from the British Library

ISBN: PB: 978-1-5266-1368-4; eBook: 978-1-5266-1370-7

2 4 6 8 10 9 7 5 3

Text design by Jeanette Levy
Typeset by Westchester Publishing Services

Printed and bound in Great Britain by CPI Group (UK) Ltd, Croydon CR0 4YY

To find out more about our authors and books visit www.bloomsbury.com
and sign up for our newsletters

In loving memory of my grandparents
Roberta Cooke & James Edward Cooke Sr.

"New York City is no place for a little girl," Mom says. "I don't think Amara is ready to visit." She takes plates from the cabinet, getting ready for the dinner Dad is cooking.

I am sitting at the kitchen island, reading, sort of . . . I have been on the same page for the past fifteen minutes because instead of reading I am listening to Mom and Dad's conversation.

I am irritated for a couple of reasons. One, because the "little girl" she is referring to is me—except I am *not* a little girl. Exactly two weeks and one day from today, I will be twelve years old. And besides, it's not like there aren't hundreds, actually thousands—maybe even hundreds of thousands—of kids who live in New York City. I asked if I could go for my birthday to visit Dad's family, and it set off this long "discussion."

Mom says, "Kids who are born and raised in New York City is one thing. Kids from Oregon visiting is another." She keeps listing reasons why letting me visit New York is a bad idea. She says to Dad, "We don't even let Amara walk to school alone. How is she going to navigate a big city? Amara doesn't know anything about a place like New York. She's lived in the suburbs her whole life."

As if Dad doesn't know where I was born, where I live.

We live in Beaverton, Oregon, just a thirty-minute drive from Portland. Less than that if Dad is driving. Mom always says she loves Beaverton over Portland because no matter where you are, a park is just a short walk away. There are hiking trails and bike paths tucked throughout the city. When it's not too rainy, the three of us ride our bikes and explore new routes on weekends. I like living here. It's the only place I've ever called home. But I want to see other places. Go somewhere with more people, with more things to do.

I try to catch Dad's eyes. See if he will speak up for me and convince Mom to let me go to New York. But he is focused on cooking. He opens the sliding door and steps outside on the patio to check the food he's grilling. He grills even when it's cold outside. He says the covered deck is why he bought this house. I think it's his favorite place to be.

I watch him take the salmon off the grill, put the fillets on a plate, and squeeze lemon on each piece. As soon as he comes back inside, I try again. "Mom, you act like Dad isn't going to be there with me. It's not like I'd be going by myself," I remind her. "Plus, I'll finally get to meet my cousins and spend time with Aunt Tracey—"

"Sweetheart, you're not going. Okay?" She puts the plates in front of me and looks at Dad like she is trying to get him to back her up.

Dad puts another dirty dish into the sink. I know Mom will fuss about that later. Dad is the best cook ever, but he uses just about every bowl, plate, knife, spoon, and fork in the kitchen by the time the meal is prepared. He cooks a big family meal once a month because most of the time he is traveling for his job or too busy to come

3

home early enough for dinner. And tomorrow morning Dad is leaving for LA, which means Mom and I will be eating takeout for the next few days.

Mom eyes all the dirty dishes in the sink. "Babe, you're going to have to wash those. You can't leave this mess for Hannah to clean."

"Don't we pay Hannah to clean the house?" Dad asks.

Mom lets out a sigh, and I know this means she has had enough with both me and Dad. I get up and take the plates over to set the table, the one in the kitchen. We mostly eat in here instead of the formal dining room. We only eat there on Thanksgiving or when guests are joining us. Right now, it's an extension of Mom's workroom. Her sketches, along with fashion magazines and swatches of fabric, are spread across the table. Mom designs dresses and sells them at her boutique in downtown Portland's Pearl District. It's called Amara's Closet, which I know sounds amazing to most people—especially my friends—I mean, none of them have a whole clothing line and store named after them, but since there's nothing in that boutique I'd actually wear, it's not that big a deal to me.

I'd much rather wear the clothes Dad gets for me. He's the vice president of sports marketing at Nike and oversees

4

branding and special events like the annual All-Star basketball games and the launching of new shoes. Sometimes Dad brings me shoes that aren't even in stores yet. But mostly, I just rotate my Air Jordan Retro collection. I have one through twelve, but my favorite is the AJ4. I get those every time they come out.

As Dad takes the pan of roasted potatoes out of the oven and brings it to the table, Mom says, "I just don't want her going to New York yet."

Here's another thing that's irritating about this conversation. Mom is talking about me like I'm not in the kitchen. Like she didn't just walk past me—her actual daughter—who can hear everything she's saying.

"Maybe when she's older," she says.

I clear my throat. "Like twelve?" I ask. "You've been asking what I want for my birthday—well, this is what I want. A trip to New York. Dad is going for the All-Star Game. Why can't I go with him?"

"He's going for work, Amara," Mom says.

Before I can object, Dad gives me a look telling me to let it go. He sprinkles a little salt into the bowl of broccoli and says, "Dinner's ready." We sit at the table, and Dad prays over the food. "We thank you, God, not only for this

5

food, but for this family. Bless us, and keep us, and please—"

"Let me go to New York with Dad to meet Dad's side of the family," I blurt out.

Dad opens one eye, Mom opens both. We all say, "Amen."

Dad passes the plate of salmon first, then the potatoes, then the broccoli. I reach for the basket of homemade dinner rolls and pass it. I swallow my first bite and take a deep breath just as Mom says, "We're not going to talk about this all night, Amara."

How did she know I was going to say something else? I put down my fork. "Can I just say one more thing?" I ask.

Both Mom and Dad answer at the same time, Dad saying *yes*, Mom saying *no*. Mom gives in. "Go ahead."

"I just want to meet the family I've only seen in pictures," I say. "And you both keep saying that once the baby comes Dad won't be traveling as much, so I think I should go now."

At the mention of the baby, Mom touches her belly. Dad and Mom give each other a look.

I knew I'd get them with that. Bringing up the new addition to our family always gets them. Just about every

6

other sentence out of their mouths begins with, "Well, you know, once the baby comes we're not going to be able to . . ." and usually what they're not going to be able to do is something I love to do, so I'm thinking this little baby is already messing up my life and she is not even born yet.

Mom says, "Amara, the answer is no. You are not going to New York for your birthday, so you need to come up with something else you want to do." She drinks from her glass of water and then says, "And you can stop asking, okay?" She rubs her belly again, and I wonder about the little life inside her.

I haven't told anyone this, but I don't want Mom and Dad to have another baby. I feel bad for admitting it, especially after all the babies Mom was pregnant with and then lost. When I was younger, I really, *really* wanted a little brother or sister, but after so many times of wishing and hoping only to have no little brother or sister, I just stopped wanting one. But then, Mom and Dad told me they were expecting (again). I just said okay and walked away, and I didn't wish or hope, or think of names, or talk to Mom's belly at all. But this time, the little baby inside Mom kept growing and growing, and in a month Mom is supposed to have my baby sister. Mom takes the last bite of her

7

dinner roll and pushes her plate back. "Babe, that was so good. Nothing like fresh baked bread."

"Thanks. My mother's recipe," Dad says.

Grandma Grace died before I could meet her. I love it when Dad cooks from her recipes. Makes me feel like she is here with us, that she is giving us love. Thinking about her makes me think of New York again and how if I could just go to Harlem, I could learn more about Grandma Grace. If I could see the home my dad grew up in, I could stand in her kitchen. I eat another bite and then say, "Mom, what if we *all* go to New York? Maybe not for my birthday . . . but what about after the baby is born?"

Dad laughs. "You have my persistence, that's for sure."

Mom shakes her head. "And you say that like it's a good thing."

"Now, let's not knock persistence. It got me a yes from *you*," Dad says. He kisses Mom on her cheek and smiles at me. "Your mom was not feeling me at all when we first met."

"Why not?"

"It wasn't him that I wasn't feeling. It was his city," Mom says. "New York is dirty, crowded, either too hot or too cold, and ridiculously expensive."

"Hey, you're talking about my hometown."

"Sorry, honey, but you know I'm telling the truth." Mom turns to me, says, "Besides, Amara, I only went to New York for college, and I knew once I graduated I'd be coming back to Oregon. I didn't want to get involved with someone who was going to try to make me stay."

"But little did she know I was ready for a change and wanted to leave the city," Dad says. "Plus my dream job was to work at Nike, so I had already looked into moving to Beaverton. Once I told her that, I had her attention. But I still had to convince her to go on a date with me."

Mom smiles. "He tried hard, too, Amara. Reciting me poems and everything."

"Poems? Dad reciting poems?"

Dad gets up from the table. "Okay, all right. Enough about me."

I take that to mean we can go back to talking about my trip to New York. I look at Mom and ask, "So is this your way of telling me that if I stay persistent and recite you a poem, then you'll let me go?"

Mom gives me that look, the one that says she's had enough and I better get myself together before I regret it. I don't get the look often. A few times she's given it to me when she's already told me two or three times to turn the TV off and get my homework done.

I let it go.

I get up, put my plate in the dishwasher, and excuse myself to my room. As I walk away Mom says, "Homework first."

"I know," I tell her.

On the way to my bedroom, I hear Mom say to Dad, "You love making me be the bad guy, huh? Now why you got that girl thinking she can go to Harlem with you? You haven't seen or talked to your father in about twelve years. You really think it's appropriate for Amara to be there when you finally do see him?"

My hand is on the doorknob, but I don't open the door. I stand real still so they don't know I'm in the hallway listening.

Dad says, "Going to Harlem doesn't mean I have to see my dad. I've been to New York several times in the past few years. They don't need to know when I'm back in the city."

"But I think for Amara the whole point is to meet your—"

"Leslie, not now. Please."

I go into my room, sit on my bed.

My father hasn't talked with Grandpa Earl in twelve years?

He's actually been in New York City and didn't go home? I know he's been for work, but still. How do you not talk to your father, and why didn't I know this?

Dad hasn't talked with Grandpa Earl, but I have. I talk to Grandpa Earl every Father's Day and on Thanksgiving and Christmas and on my birthday and his birthday. I've never really thought about it before, but now that I am remembering, every time I talk to Grandpa Earl it's Mom who calls me to the phone. When I am finished, I give the phone back to Mom. I think and think, but I can't remember a time when I saw or heard Dad on the phone with Grandpa Earl. He talks with Aunt Tracey a lot. She's been here, to Beaverton, to visit us a few times. Sometimes Dad sends shoes to my cousins, Nina and Ava, but he doesn't speak with Grandpa Earl.

I think maybe I've had it all wrong. Mom is not the one I need to convince about me taking a trip to Harlem. Dad is.

Mom knocks on my door an hour later. "Is your home-work finished?" She comes inside.

"Yes," I say. I close my book, put it on the nightstand.

Mom sits on my bed, rubbing her stomach. "She's kicking. Want to feel?"

"That's okay," I answer. I do not want to feel a baby who may not actually be born. Mom is eight months preg-nant now, and everyone says that means this baby is sure to come. But three times we decorated nurseries. Three times she told me, "You're going to have to get ready to be a big sister."

Three times it was a lie.

And she never, ever talked about it except to say, "It just wasn't meant to be."

Mom stands and goes over to my walk-in closet. She has hung bundles of lavender in the corners, and every time the door opens, my room smells like spring. She looks at my shelves and picks up the Jason Markk kit Dad bought me to clean my sneakers. "When I was your age an old toothbrush, detergent, and warm water did the trick. I guess this makes you a bona fide sneakerhead, huh?"

"Yep. Just like Dad."

Mom searches through the hanging clothes and goes to the end of the row. "Have you tried on the dresses I made for you?"

"They don't fit."

Mom gives me her I-Know-You're-Lying look. "You don't have to wear the dresses every day. They're for church," she says.

"Why can't we go to a church that lets women wear pants, like Titus's church?" I ask. Titus is my best friend. He lives around the corner. His dad works with my dad, and our families are together all the time. Whenever Dad and Big T—Titus Sr.—get together, all they talk about is how New York and Oregon are so different. Big T is from Harlem, like Dad, and they became friends when they were students at New York University. Big T starts just about every sentence with, "Well, in Harlem . . ." Mostly he talks about missing black culture. He drives from Beaverton all the way to Portland because he wants to go to a black barbershop. He's always talking about how he misses black people, which makes me wonder why he moved to Oregon. Big T says if it weren't for Dad, he might not have graduated and would've never moved across the country to do what he loves, which is design shoes.

I give Mom my best reasons for why going to church with Titus's family would be way better than going to our church. "Besides being able to wear pants, their service is only an hour," I say.

Mom shakes her head. "How long the service is and what you can or can't wear is not important. I grew up in that church, and I like Pastor Franklin's preaching. Plus, wearing a dress once a week isn't going to hurt you," Mom says. She fans through the hanging clothes and picks out the two new dresses she made. One is a shirtdress with big pockets and looks casual enough to wear to school with

14

leggings, but also appropriate for church, depending on what shoes I wear with it. I guess it's not so bad. It's better than the second dress, which has a busy print with at least five colors. It looks like the kind of dress that wrinkles if you do the tiniest movement, like raise your hand or bend over. It's the kind of dress that makes people say, "Oh, you're so beautiful," or "You're such a pretty girl." No one ever says that when I am wearing jeans and a T-shirt.

"I just think church shouldn't be all about what a person is wearing on the outside. It's what they believe on the inside," I say.

"And I agree," Mom tells me. "I also believe that what you look like on the outside is a reflection of who you are. And how you dress going anywhere—school, church, or even the mall for that matter—shows how much you respect yourself or a place. Dressing up for church is showing that you care about where you're going, that this one day out of the week is special enough for you not to wear your everyday clothes because you are going to honor God." Mom is always good with a comeback. "There's a time and place for everything. I don't expect you to wear a ball gown to a basketball game, just like I don't think it's appropriate to wear shorts in the sanctuary." Mom holds the dresses up in the air, toward the light, and looks them over. "Here. Humor me, at least." She hands me both dresses. "Try these on."

I change into the colorful one first, so that way when I tell her how much I don't like it but how much I like the other one, we'll end this fitting on a good note. Mom fusses over me, turning me around in circles so she can see me from different angles. She gently directs me to the full-length mirror in my closet. "See, this looks so good on you, Amara."

"But, Mom, I'm uncomfortable in it."

"Does it feel too tight?" she asks. "It doesn't look tight at all."

"No, it's not tight," I tell her. But it is suffocating me. "Mom, you know I don't like dresses."

"But you look so pretty in them," Mom says.

I look into the mirror with Mom behind me waiting for me to change my mind. I stay silent until she sighs and says, "Well, take it off."

I pull the dress off and reach for the other dress, which is now hanging on Mom's left arm. She holds on to both dresses, like she is rescuing them from a dangerous place.

"I'll try that one on," I say, pointing to the shirtdress. I think I'll wear it to school tomorrow—to make her see I am willing to compromise. "I like that one."

"No, it's okay, Amara. I don't want to make you do anything you don't want to do." She folds the dresses. "You know most girls your age would love to have one-of-a-kind clothes designed especially for them," she says. "When I was a little girl I loved wearing dresses. I'd sneak in my mother's closet and play dress up in her clothes, strutting around in her high heel shoes. I don't know whose child you are."

When she says this I feel like what she is saying is that I am not girl enough, daughter enough, that I am nothing like her. I look at Mom's belly, think maybe it's a great thing she's having a baby. Maybe she'll have the daughter she's always wanted. A girl nothing like me.

"You know, you used to like wearing the clothes I made for you," Mom says.

That was in elementary school when I didn't have much of a choice, when I didn't mind being a mini version of Mom, her look-alike, real-life doll. But the older I get, the less I am like Mom. The more I am like me.

17

Weekday mornings usually start with Mom and Dad at the kitchen table reading the morning paper over hot cups of coffee. I am always awake before Mom calls out to me, but I like to stay in bed till the absolute last minute I have to get up. Today, my bedroom door creaks open before daylight rises and there's no aroma of coffee floating to my room. I remember that today is not an ordinary morning. Dad is leaving for his trip.

Dad whispers, "Amara? Amara?"

I sit up in my bed, eyes squinting, trying to focus in the darkness.

"I just want to say goodbye before I leave." He kisses me on my forehead.

"When do you get back?" I ask.

"Quick trip. I get back Sunday night."

"Sunday night?" I am wide awake now. "But what about taking me to the Nike Employee Store?"

"Oh, I . . . sorry, sweetheart. Your mom will have to take you," Dad says.

"Dad—"

"Amara, my flight doesn't get in till Sunday night. Nothing I can do about that. Your mom knows how to get there."

That is not the point. At all. New Nikes come out every Saturday at the Employee Store, and Dad and I go together whenever there's a release that I really, really want. We get up at five o'clock in the morning, and our first stop is the McDonald's drive-through. We order the same thing every time—two Sausage, Egg, and Cheese McGriddles and two hash browns. Dad gets coffee, I get orange juice. This is our thing. We eat breakfast in the car and then drive to the Employee Store to get in the line that—by the time we get there—is just starting to wrap around the building. The die-hard shoe lovers who've gotten special passes to come to the store usually get there around three o'clock in the morning. The store doesn't open until ten o'clock. We've done this in summer heat, in the rain, during winter months when it is still dark out when we leave. Sometimes it feels like we are sneaking out of the house to go on a private, secret mission. There's no way Mom is going to do this. She won't want to wait in line that long, and by the time we go, there won't be any shoes left.

Dad kisses me on my forehead again. "I'm sorry," he says. "Love you."

"Love you, too."

Before leaving for school, I check my weather app to see the forecast. The weather determines what shoes I'll wear. It's going to rain today, so I put on my all-black Jordan 1's with the pink swoosh. I leave for school and meet Titus at the end of the block. As we walk, I tell Titus all about my plan to get Mom and Dad to change their minds about me going to Harlem. "I think I almost won them over when I mentioned the baby. I just need to keep bringing that up— that once the baby is here Dad won't be able to travel much because Mom will need him, and me, I guess, but mostly my dad."

"I don't think that's going to help your case. If it didn't make her change her mind when you first said it, she's not going to change it the second, third, or fourth time," Titus tells me. "Plus, your dad travels for work. He's always going to be traveling."

"Well, thanks for the encouragement," I say.

"I'm just being honest. Let's try to think of something else, something that will really tug at her heart," Titus says.

I can tell he is thinking hard. We walk half a block without saying anything, and then he blurts out, "I got it!" Titus switches his backpack from his left to right shoulder. "What if you promise your mom that you'll do a report or something on Harlem. Like, maybe if you go and visit all the famous places of the Harlem Renaissance you can—"

"I am not going to give myself an assignment. Not going to happen." We walk down the hill and cross the street. "That's the worst idea ever, Titus. Homework? I want to go and have *fun*, not do research."

"Well, my idea is better than using your baby sister as a reason," he says.

"Let's just, let's keep thinking," I say.

Titus sighs. "I think that was my best idea. I can't think of anything else."

"Me neither," I say. But I think Titus isn't trying as hard because he visits New York all the time with his dad, so maybe he doesn't realize what a big deal it is that I have never been.

The clouds shift and the rain begins to drip, drip. First a drizzle but by the time we make it to the end of the block, it is pouring. We usually cut through the small park to get to school, but Titus asks, "Can we go that way?" pointing to the sidewalk. "Can't get these muddy."

And Mom thinks I'm the sneakerhead.

We take the long way, with Titus walking more zigzag than straight to avoid deep puddles. We don't say much until we're about a block from school. As we turn the corner, I ask Titus, "Do you think it's weird for someone to stop talking to their parent?"

"Are you *that* mad at your mom? I doubt the silent treatment will do anything but get you in trouble."

"No, not me. My dad. I found out last night that he hasn't talked to my grandpa for twelve years."

"Twelve years?" Titus asks. "Whoa. Something really bad must have happened."

We cross the street and pass the line of cars parked along the drop-off area. Parents are waving goodbye, and car doors are slamming shut. The younger kids wobble to their side of campus, on the right. The middle school students funnel into our building. When I enter the building, I take my wet coat off and stomp my feet on the mat at the door. Titus heads toward his homeroom. "See you at lunch," he says.

I say goodbye and head to my humanities class. Mr. Rosen is at the door greeting everyone as we walk in. On the way to my desk I notice there are vintage suitcases all over the classroom: some on the floor under the dry-erase board, some lined up against the back wall, and a few on top of the file cabinets.

Mr. Rosen says, "Today, we're starting a new unit, the Suitcase Project. You'll be creating time capsules that explore your past, present, and future. At the end of the semester, you each will decorate a suitcase with personal artifacts, poems, and essays about where you're from and what your dreams are for the future."

As he talks, I set my eyes on the suitcase on top of the cabinet. It's wood and leather with a cherry finish. That's the one I want. It reminds me of a mini version of the chest upstairs in the attic, the one I've never seen Mom or Dad open.

The chest is a sacred thing. When I was younger, I used to pretend that it was a magic box and that if I opened it, it would take me to a faraway place. Once, when I had friends over on a rainy indoor play day, I realized it was the perfect spot for hiding during a game of hide-and-seek. I bundled my legs under my body, ducked down behind it, and disappeared. But I got in trouble for that because Mom said I shouldn't be playing around precious things. I couldn't understand what the big deal was. If it is so precious why was it hidden in a cold, dark place? I still wonder what's in it.

Mr. Rosen has given each of us a packet with prompts for writing about our family history. One of the pages has guidelines for creating self-portraits, timelines, and choosing artifacts and photos to include in the suitcase. "You'll notice you'll have to interview at least two important adults in your life and create an essay based off your interviews. I'd like you to be creative with this," Mr. Rosen says.

Annabelle raises her hand and asks, "What do you mean by artifacts?"

"Think of it as family keepsakes, items in your life that have a special story to them."

Annabelle asks, "You mean like my mother's wedding ring?"

"It's your mom's ring, not yours. That wouldn't count," Benjamin blurts out.

Mr. Rosen says, "Well, that would count actually. I'm sure there's a special story behind it, right, Annabelle?"

"It was my grandmother's ring, and my great-grandmother's, too. It'll be mine one day because I'm the first granddaughter."

"This is a perfect example." Mr. Rosen bends over, picks up one of the suitcases, and opens it. "Now, I wouldn't expect you to put the ring in here, but a photo of it or even a poem about it is what I'm looking for," he explains. "You could paste your poem on the inside and make your own lining."

Annabelle looks all proud, like she already has a plan for her suitcase. But me? I don't have any stories to tell about my family. I raise my hand. "But what if you don't have any special artifacts to take a picture of?"

"Yeah," Benjamin says. "It'll be impossible for me to get a good grade."

I'm glad I'm not the only one who feels like this assignment is impossible. Mom is an only child, and both her parents have passed away. Dad hardly ever talks about his family. So I don't know how full my suitcase will be.

"First, let me say that I think you'll be surprised at what you'll learn about your family just by asking for the story behind a photo, or blanket, or something as simple as a chair," Mr. Rosen says. "Everything and everyone has a story, a beginning." Mr. Rosen closes the suitcase and latches the lock. He looks at us, and I think he can see that most of us are anxious. "There's no wrong way to do this. You just have to ask questions of your loved ones and document what they tell you." Mr. Rosen tells us that our suitcases will be on display at the school-wide spring festival. "And the more creative, the better. Maybe your suitcase carries actual, tangible items. But some things you won't be able to put in your suitcase; some things are intangible, and yet, you carry them with you. Think about how you will represent the places you come from, the people who are important to you."

I look through the packet and read some of the prompts: *Interview a family member about their childhood. Make a list of family traditions. Write a poem about all the places you are connected to.*

I can do this. Maybe it won't be so bad after all.

Mr. Rosen ends class by telling us, "This project isn't about who can make the coolest suitcase display. It's about the question, not the answer. The journey, not the destination."

The bell rings, and Titus meets me in the hallway. We head toward Ms. Sutton's math class. Ms. Sutton is one of my favorite teachers. She makes math fun and interesting. This is the first year I've actually felt confident doing math and not anxious or intimidated. As we walk down to Ms. Sutton's room, Titus goes on and on about the Legends event at the Nike campus and how we should get there early if we want to hear Michael Jordan speak. "Are you even listening to me?" Titus asks.

I am. Kind of. But mostly I am thinking about the Suitcase Project. All that talk about family and history, journey and destination has me thinking about Dad and Harlem. Dad and Grandpa Earl. I am thinking about how amazing it would be to go to Harlem so I can work on the assignment there—collecting keepsakes for my suitcase, interviewing Grandpa Earl. Maybe if I tell Mom about the Suitcase Project she'll let me go.

"Uh, are you really going to act like meeting *the* Michael Jordan isn't a big deal?" Titus says.

"Sorry, yes—of course. It's the biggest deal."

"Well, you sure aren't acting like it."

I tell Titus about Mr. Rosen's assignment and my new plan to convince Mom to let me go to New York.

Titus says, "See—homework *is* the way to change her mind." He'll never let it go that he was right the first time. "If that doesn't work, nothing will." Then he tells me: "You could even ask to get extra credit. I mean, you'll be one of the only students who can *literally* say what your suitcase carries." As we enter math class, Titus adds, "Plus your parents will have to answer all your questions since it's for homework. You can ask your dad what happened twelve years ago."

I sit down, take my math book out of my backpack. I already know the answer to that question. Twelve years ago, I was born.

When I get home after school, I look around my house and think about what Mr. Rosen said. *Everything and everyone has a story.* The more I think, the more I realize there's so much I don't know about my family, this house. I look around the living room, wondering what more there is to know about the photos caged behind the frames. Those photos have a story, and so do the curtains, and the Crock-Pot in the kitchen. I do not know the story of Mom's china. Was it a gift on her wedding day or something she splurged on? Is the knitted blanket I've seen tossed over the armchair my entire eleven (almost twelve) years handmade by someone special?

All this stuff holding memories, all these unspoken histories around me. I sit on the sofa and look at the over-sized Bible in the middle of the coffee table. None of us ever read it. But it is always open evenly down the middle, just sitting there untouched. Hannah dusts around it, handling it like it is made of glass.

That Bible has a story, I'm sure.

For the first time in my eleven (almost twelve) years, I pick it up. It isn't something that can be held in one hand. I carry it in my arms and sit on the sofa and flip the thin pages to the beginning. The first page says *Holy Bible King James Version*, and then there are blank pages until I turn to a page that has gold lettering at the top that says Presented To. My parents' names are written underneath in black ink. The handwriting swirls and curls like the ringlets in Mom's freshly washed hair. I turn the page, and there's more gold lettering that says Family Record. There's space to write down marriages, births, and baptisms. Mom's handwriting has filled out some of the lines. Her birth date, Dad's, and mine. The date I was baptized is written down, too. But there are so many blank lines just waiting for the names of my baby brothers and sisters.

At the bottom of the page, the last section is for recording deaths. If it were up to me, no names would ever be written on these lines. But it is already too late because Mom has written down the names of her mom and dad and the dates they died. Under their names, I see Grandma Grace's name. I am not surprised to see her name there, but what startles me is the date beside it.

My birth date.

Grandma Grace died on the day I was born.

I put the Bible back on the coffee table. Maybe it's good I don't know everything about our family. Maybe Mom and Dad don't talk about the past for a reason. I walk upstairs, head to my room. I can tell that Hannah has been here. The house smells like lemons, and I can hear the *chug, chug, chug* of the dishwasher. I go into the nursery and notice that Mom has added more to it. The crib and changing table are dark brown, and the blanket that drapes the old-fashioned rocking chair is a soft gray and yellow. Mom and Dad said they didn't care what they had as long as the baby was healthy, but I see the joy in Mom's eyes every time someone asks her what she's having and she says, "A girl."

My mind shifts from one thought to another—Will my baby sister capture Mom's heart, making Mom love me less? Why did Dad and Grandpa stop talking? Was it because of me?

I leave the nursery and go to my room. I've got homework, and I know when Mom gets home from the boutique, the first question she is going to ask me is have I finished it yet. My bedroom is reorganized—not that it was that messy or anything. It's just that Hannah likes everything in its place. She's rearranged my books and shelved them by size on the bookcase, and my bed looks so perfect, so neat, that I don't want to sit on it.

I try to focus, get started on my math. I am on the third equation when Mom gets home. She calls to me, and I go downstairs. She has takeout from our favorite Thai restaurant. I unpack the bag and dish out the massaman curry and white rice while she grabs silverware. Mom must be really hungry because she isn't even at the table yet when she prays, "Lord, thank you for this food. Bless it in Jesus's name. Amen." She gets two glasses out of the cabinet and pours the large Thai tea into both until they are even.

I start eating. "Thanks, Mom."

"Mmm-hmm," she mumbles with her mouth full. We chew and swallow, sip and repeat for a while without talking, then Mom puts her fork down and does this thing she always does where she asks me a question she already knows the answer to. Like when the doorbell rings and she says, "You want to get that?" when she knows I don't feel like getting up from the most comfortable sofa. Or when she looks at my unfinished plate of food—with everything eaten except the vegetables—and she says, "Are you finished?" That's how she is, so when she asks me, "Have you thought about what you want to do for your birthday?" I don't even answer. She knows exactly what I want for my birthday.

"I was thinking you could have a sleepover, and we can ask Sierra's mom if she can come over and give you girls manicures," she says. "I know she does home spa parties for special events. Would you like that?"

"Sure," I say. I actually like this idea. Getting manicures is something Mom and I do together every two weeks. Mom always knows beforehand what color she is going to get, but I have to look over all the options before I can decide. I wonder if my little sister will like to come with us. If we'll make it an all-girls outing, leaving Dad at home.

"Let me know who's on the guest list so I can send invitations out," Mom says. "I'll call Sierra's mom tomorrow."

We finish eating but stay at the table talking. "So, how's school?" Mom asks.

"School is okay."

"Just okay?"

I tell Mom about the Suitcase Project.

"That sounds fun." Mom stands and starts clearing the table. She puts our forks and glasses in the dishwasher and grabs a dishcloth to wipe down the table.

"I wouldn't say fun—"

"Why not?"

"Well, I don't know what to write about because I don't know anything about our family."

"Amara, that's not true. You know my parents were born in Louisiana, that I was their only child and—"

"I know the facts, Mom. I'm asking for some stories. Like, what happened in our family? What should I know about where I come from?"

I help Mom clean by throwing the takeout cartons in the trash. Once we're finished in the kitchen, we go into the living room. I think we are going to find a movie to watch, but instead Mom says, "You know, I'm glad you have to do this project. I think it will be good for you—for all of us. Sometimes things happen in a family that are painful and hard and no one knows how or when to talk about it so we just, well, we don't talk."

"So, you're saying you and Dad keep family secrets?"

"We're not trying to keep secrets, sweetheart. It's just that some stories are hard to tell," Mom says.

Like how Grandma died on the day I was born, I think to myself. I don't say it out loud. I don't want to bring up something that will make Mom sad. As bad as I want to know about my family history, I don't want to know if I am the reason why Dad and Grandpa Earl don't talk anymore. Maybe there are some stories that should never be retold. Maybe.

"So, how can I help you with your project?" Mom asks. "What do you want to know?"

Here's my chance to ask anything, and I can't think of what to say. Well, I can think of a million questions, but I just want to ask the right one, the one that isn't so hard to talk about. I say, "Tell me about Grandma Grace."

Mom's whole face brightens. "She was a strong, thoughtful, wise woman. That's why we named you after her. Amara means 'grace,' and we wanted you to have her essence. And you certainly do."

Mom tells me how Grandma Grace liked to cook, how she was the peacemaker in the family. "And oh, Amara, you would have loved going to basketball games with her. Your grandpa Earl used to be one of the assistant coaches for the Knicks. And your grandma Grace was his biggest fan. When she went to games, I think she cheered more for your grandpa than the players." Mom laughs and I do, too.

"I didn't know Grandpa Earl was a coach."

Mom looks at me like she is not sure I am right about what I do and don't know. "Really?"

"I'm positive," I say. "See—secrets. And this isn't even something so bad you need to hide it."

"Amara, it's not a secret. It's, it's just—there was a whole life going on before you were born. You know? I've had a whole childhood, your dad has. We've gone to schools, had jobs, had heartbreaks and so much joy. There's a lot that happened before you got here, and I think some things just get forgotten or aren't mentioned because life keeps on moving and we're creating new memories with you, not realizing we haven't shared old ones. Does that make sense?"

"I guess," I say.

Mom keeps going with stories about Grandma Grace. She tells me that when her own mother died, Grandma Grace really took Mom in as her own daughter. With each story I feel more and more connected to Grandma Grace. Mom says I have her laugh, her smile, her love of books. She says that I am a steady reminder that Grandma Grace is still here. Inside me.

5

I wake up at 4:30 the next morning. My eyes are stinging with tiredness, and they don't really want to be open, but I know that while I am lying here in this warm, cozy bed, there's a line wrapping around Nike. I get up and I'm dressed and ready in less than ten minutes—teeth brushed and all. I walk down the hall to Mom and Dad's room. I knock twice before deciding to go in. "Mom?"

She turns over.

"Mom, you have to wake up. It's time to go."

She groans.

"Mom, you promised you'd take me."

"Amara, honey, I know. But this baby and Thai food did not agree. I was up all night. I can't right now—I just . . . Give me a few hours."

"A few hours? Mom—there's no point in going if we don't go early."

Mom turns on her side, bends a pillow under her head. *"Mom."*

"Amara, I'm not saying no. I'm saying not right now."

"That is saying no. If we don't go now, by the time we get there my size will be gone. I'm not going to get—"

"Amara Baker!"

I stop begging. Switch up my strategy. "Well, can I order them on the SNKRS app?"

"Do you get the employee discount on the app?"

"No, but—"

"We'll go later. Close the door, please."

I go to my room, text Titus to ask if he is going. Knowing Titus, he is already there, but either he doesn't have his phone with him or he has it and it's not charged. I get back in bed, but now that I've been up, I can't go to sleep.

I wait.

Every now and then I can hear a car driving down the

street, the tires demolishing puddles. Every thirty minutes I go to Mom's bedroom and hold my ear up to the door.

5:00. She's still sleeping.

5:30. She's still sleeping.

6:00. She's still sleeping.

6:30. Still.

And then at 7:00 I hear Mom walking down the hallway, down the stairs.

I run downstairs. "You ready?" I ask.

Mom is at the stove scrambling eggs.

"Mom—we don't have time for that."

"There's always time for breakfast," Mom says. "These eggs will be ready in two minutes."

I should just say never mind. Should just say let's spend our Saturday morning doing something else, because I know there is no way I'm going to get shoes today. We finally get in the car and make our way to the Employee Store. Once we turn onto Knowlton Street, I can already see this is going to be even worse than I thought. Traffic is backed up so bad we can't even pull into the parking lot. The first thing Mom says is, "All of this for some shoes? This is ridiculous."

I don't even bother to remind her that if we had come earlier, we wouldn't have to wait in traffic. Once we're in the parking lot we circle it at a snail's pace to find a spot. Nothing. Just when Mom calls it quits, I see Titus walking out of the store with one bag in his left hand and one in his right.

Mom rolls her window down and the cold air rushes in. "Big T," she yells. "I see you got in. Where'd you park? I'll follow you."

"Nothing in there now. Might as well go home, unless you coming to get some headbands or shoelaces." He's laughing, but I don't think it's funny at all. Then he nudges Titus and says, "But Titus hooked Amara up."

Titus walks to the passenger side of the car. I roll my window down. "Size eight, right?" He hands me the bag in his right hand.

Mom erupts in gratitude. "Aw, you didn't have to do that. That is so nice of you."

She goes on and on so much, I can hardly get my own thank-you out.

Titus says, "When my dad told me your father was out of town I kind of figured you weren't coming."

"Oh, your dad told you? I sent you a text this morning."

Titus takes his phone out of his pocket. "Oh, my battery is dead."

I open the bag and there they are. The newest pair of Jordans. "Thank you, Titus."

"You're welcome."

Mom says to Big T, "How much do I owe you?"

"Come on now," he says. "You already know—you don't owe me anything." He steps away from the car, refusing to take any money. A horn honks, and Big T motions for Titus to come over to him. "Look at us holding people up. We better let you go." They walk away.

"Thanks, Big T. Thanks, Titus," I shout out the window.

Titus smiles at me, and as soon as we drive off, Mom says, "See, it all worked out."

I want to ask if we can stop at McDonald's on the way home, but I figure I can't have it all.

Mom and I are at the dining room table, which is actually cleaned off, filling out the invitations for my birthday sleepover. I have a stack, and she has a stack. Even our handwriting is opposite, hers more like pearls, mine like hoop earrings. "Mom?" I ask. "Am I the reason Dad and Grandpa Earl stopped talking?" I didn't plan on asking, not right now, but I can't stop thinking about what I saw in that Bible, what I heard Mom and Dad talking about.

Mom sets her pen down. "Absolutely not, sweetheart. Why would you think that?"

"I overheard you and Dad." I say "overheard" because it sounds better than telling her I was eavesdropping. "I know Grandma Grace died the day I was born, and I know Dad and Grandpa Earl stopped talking twelve years ago."

"Amara, no. Your dad and Grandpa Earl have some things to work through, but it has nothing to do with you."

I want to believe her. "Why aren't they talking?" I ask.

Mom thinks for a moment, then says, "That's your dad's story to tell." She gets up from the table and goes to the built-in bookshelf next to the fireplace. She takes a photo box from the bottom shelf, opens the lid, and says, "But I can tell you some of *my* stories." Mom spreads photos and letters, postcards and greeting cards all over the table. I pick up a card that has one small red heart in the middle of it. When I open it, I recognize Dad's handwriting right away. "I can read this?" I ask just to make sure.

"Yes, you can look through all of this. You know, before texts and emails and FaceTime, there was just good old-fashioned handwriting on paper," Mom says. "Maybe you'll find something useful for your project."

I look through Mom's pile of memories: photos of Mom when she was a baby nestled in her mother's arms, postcards from her college friends, cards from Aunt Tracey.

Mom walks into the kitchen, where she left her cell phone, and calls out to me, "What do you think about pizza for dinner?"

"Ah, yeah, sure." I can't even think about eating right now. I am full from the feast spread out on this table.

6

Dad is missing church, and I can't wait until he gets home tonight to tell him that Mom and I actually went to Titus's church. He is going to be so disappointed, mostly because at Titus's church they serve coffee and doughnuts in the foyer. When Mom and I walk in the building, an usher who is wearing a black T-shirt and jeans says, "Welcome, and help yourself to our coffee corner." I walk over to the long tables that are covered with trays of doughnuts, muffins, and scones. There are three black dispensers on the table: one for coffee, another for decaf coffee, and the last one full of hot water for tea and hot cocoa drinkers. "What do you want, Mom?"

"Nothing. We just ate at home," Mom says. "Plus, I can't gulp down hot coffee. Church will be starting soon, and we can't take food into the sanctuary."

I point to the man who is walking into the sanctuary with his own travel mug of coffee. "I don't think it matters if you drink in the sanctuary," I say.

Behind him is a woman carrying tea in one hand and a scone wrapped in a napkin.

"Are we at church or the movies?" Mom asks.

"Mom."

"Come, on, let's go in." Mom puts her arm around me, guiding me inside.

"But can't I get a doughnut?"

"Look, I see they have different norms here, but you know this is not what we do." We walk past the pews in the back and see Titus and his family sitting on the left side near the middle. Titus's mom waves us over. I call her Aunt Sofie, even though she is not my real aunt. She's like a sister to Mom, so that makes her family. I wish Mom was close to Aunt Tracey, my real aunt. Wish I could know what it's like to go to church with her and my cousins. We slide into the pew, stepping over feet and bags that are on the floor, and sit down with them.

Titus looks like he looks at school—jeans and a hoodie. Big T and Aunt Sofie are a little more dressed up but not by much. They both look like they'd be comfortable if we all decided to go to the movies after church. But not me or Mom. My feet hurt in these pointy shoes, and Mom would definitely be overdressed if she went to a theater looking like that. No matter how much I told Mom that Titus's church was casual, she insisted on us wearing the clothes we always wear to church. "It's what we do," she told me.

Another thing we do that is a clear difference from Titus's church is talk back to the pastor as he preaches. At my church, the congregation is always saying "Amen" and yelling out "Yes, Lord!" but not here. Here, they don't even clap after the choir sings—Mom and I both learned that the hard way. We both started clapping right after the last song, and the couple in front of us jumped—literally jumped—they were so startled. Big T gets to laughing, then Aunt Sofie and Titus get started, and Mom and I are tickled, too. This is the first time I know I won't get in trouble for laughing in church.

After church we go to dinner. After we order and are good into our meal, Big T says, "So, Amara, I hear you have a birthday coming up."

Aunt Sofie asks, "What are you doing to celebrate?"

"Well, I wanted to go to New York with my dad, but instead I'm having a slumber party." I am not trying to start a whole conversation about it, I am just telling the truth.

I couldn't have known that Big T and Aunt Sofie think me going to New York is the best idea ever. They both tell my mom, "You should let her go," but Mom is not having it. Without saying much, she just gives them a look and says, "There are many reasons why I don't think it's a good idea."

Big T can obviously read her eyes. He says, "And that might be why she should go."

Mom, Aunt Sofie, and Big T start doing what adults do—talking in code right in front of us because they don't want us kids knowing what they are talking about. So rude. I turn to Titus. "Want to go play some games?" I ask him. We leave the table and go into the game room.

I know they are talking about Dad and Grandpa and

me wanting to go visit. I know Mom is giving all her reasons why letting me go is not a good idea, but I am hoping that whatever Big T and Aunt Sofie are saying to her will change her mind.

Monday morning I wake up, and the first voice I hear is Dad's. He is in the kitchen talking with Mom in hush-hush whispers. I get dressed and ready for school and join them at the kitchen table for breakfast. When I get downstairs, I expect Dad to greet me with arms wide open and a gift from LA, like he always does whenever he comes back from a trip. But instead, he's quiet and barely looks me in the eyes. Mom too. She's sitting at the table, raking through her scrambled eggs like they're a pile of heavy rocks.

"Good morning," I say.

They both talk at the same time, slow and empty of emotion. "'Morning."

I fix my plate and sit at the table.

"How was your trip, Dad?"

He clears his throat. "It was good, yeah, it was, ah, good."

Mom gives him a look.

"What's going on?" I ask.

"You tell her," Mom says.

In an instant, every sad story I've heard from my friends about their parents sitting them down to talk floods my mind. This is either the Somebody-You-Loved-Has-Died talk or the We're-Getting-a-Divorce talk, or something else that is definitely going to ruin my day.

Mom says, "I'm sorry, Amara, but we have to cancel your birthday sleepover."

"What? Why?"

Dad says, "Because it'll be rude of you to have guests over when you're not even here." His stern face breaks into a wide smile, and he and Mom laugh and laugh. "You're going to be with me. I'm taking you to New York for your birthday."

I look at Mom. "Is he serious? Really?"

Mom is nodding. "Yes. He's serious."

"And you're letting him take me?" I ask.

"Hey, now—she's not letting me—"

"I'm letting him," Mom says. "It's only for a week. I actually think it will be good for *both of you*. We think it will be good for you to get to know your grandpa Earl and the rest of the family. And it will be good for your dad to reconnect with them."

Dad adds, "I'll be working. This is not a vacation for me."

Mom and Dad have a whole conversation with their eyes, and I don't even try to interpret it. I'm going to New York, and that's all that matters right now.

On the walk to school, the first thing I tell Titus is that I am going to Harlem to visit my dad's side of the family. "So the Suitcase Project homework assignment worked?" he asks.

"I don't think it had anything to do with that. She just, she changed her mind. She thinks I need this and that my dad does, too."

We cross the street, stopping at the median because we won't make it across this wide street before the light changes. "You should become a lawyer," Titus says. "Or a sports agent. You just negotiated with your mom and got your way. And somehow you have her thinking that this was her idea. You're good."

I laugh. "So, you have to help me come up with a must-see list," I tell Titus.

"Tourist stuff or real New York?"

"Both."

"Okay, well, there's the obvious: Times Square, Statue of Liberty. Oh, and people like to go to the top of the Empire State Building, but we like to go to the Top of the Rock. You get better photos there."

Titus bends down to tie his shoes. "And Central Park is nice, but I like Brooklyn Bridge Park better. You can see Manhattan, and other than a few couples taking wedding pictures, it's not that touristy." We cross and walk the last block to school. The sidewalk is more crowded now that we are closer to school. We weave in and out of clusters of people and make our way into the building. "I don't know. There's a lot of stuff to do." Titus says this so casual, like he is not talking about New. York. City.

"I need you to get a little more excited for me," I tell him. "You get to go to New York for whole summers. What do you do when you go back to visit?" I ask.

"We mostly stay in Harlem and visit family."

"So what should I do in Harlem?"

"You'll like 125th Street. There's a lot of shopping there. And maybe you and your cousins can go skating at Riverbank State Park," Titus tells me. "I don't know. Just whatever. It's not *that* big of a deal."

"Everything is a big deal in New York."

Titus shakes his head. "You're going to wear your dad out. I can see it now. You and him going all over the city."

"I can see it, too," I tell him. "And I can't wait."

8

This has been the longest week of my life. We leave for New York tomorrow night, and it's been torture having to wait. Mom's been fussing at me all week because every free moment I have, I've been on my phone or laptop looking up things to do and making my lists of places I want to go. I have all the things Titus suggested, plus seeing a Broadway play. But more than going to any of those places, I want to sit on the stoop of Dad's childhood home. I want to see the schools he went to, the playgrounds he played on. I want to find something to bring back for my Suitcase Project.

Mom and I are in my room packing for the trip. She's just finished oiling my scalp with coconut oil, so now my room smells like the scratch-and-sniff stickers I used to trade with Titus. He hated the smell of the coconut ones, so he always gave me his.

Mom made a list of everything I need to bring. "Don't forget to take some chewing gum in your carry-on. Just in case your ears bother you when you fly," Mom says. "And remember to bring some of those word puzzle games you like in case you get bored on the plane."

"I don't think I'll need them," I tell her. "I've packed some books."

Mom says, "Well, it's better to have them and not use them than to not have them and wish you had packed them."

Dad calls out from his office, "The plane has TV. She'll be fine."

Mom slides the word puzzles into my bag and whispers, "Just in case." She opens my closet and pulls out five sweaters. "Now, you're going to need to layer yourself. Tank top, T-shirt, sweater, scarf, coat."

"That's way too many clothes. I'm going to be too hot."

"In New York's February, there's no such thing as too

hot." Mom folds my sweaters and puts them in my suit-case. "And I bought these for you," she says, handing me five pairs of leggings. "You'll need to wear these under your jeans."

"Mom—"

"Honey, will you tell her how cold New York is in the winter?"

"Listen to your mom," Dad says. I hear his door close, and that's a signal to me and Mom that he's tired of hear-ing us fuss at each other.

Mom closes my door, too. She sits on my bed and motions for me to sit next to her. I don't know what's about to happen, but my heart starts to tremble because Mom's face looks so serious all of a sudden—not like she's annoyed with me, like a moment ago, but like she has something important to tell me. "Amara, I know you are planning on having a lot of fun. And you will. You'll remember this trip for the rest of your life. But I need you to do some-thing while you're there," she says. "I need you to make sure your dad and grandpa have some time alone. They need to talk. Now, you can't force a conversation but you can encourage them to spend quality time together. Can you do that?"

"Yes," I say. "I can do that."

After Mom leaves my room and I am in bed, not sleeping (because who can sleep the night before visiting New York City?), I lie awake thinking about what Mom asked me to do. The only other time Mom trusted me with something so important was the time she let me wear one of her necklaces made from red gems for my school's fancy Rose City Scholars Tea. She pulled the jewelry out of a velvet pouch and talked with me about how I had to take care of it, how it's only worn on special occasions. I was proud that Mom trusted me with something so precious, but it also made me nervous.

I feel that way about this trip now. Excited, but nervous, too.

When Mom takes us to the airport, I can tell she's getting emotional. "A week is a long time," she says. "I'm going to miss you two."

Dad and Mom kiss, then he puts his mouth to her stomach and says, "Be good to your mom while I'm gone. I love you." Dad rubs Mom's belly. "And I really, really love you," he says, kissing Mom's lips again.

"Okay, okay," I shout.

Mom wraps me in her arms. "Have fun, Amara, not that I have to tell you that." When she lets go, she reminds me to chew gum during the takeoff and landing and tells us to call her as soon as the plane lands. "Call, not text," she says.

Dad and I walk into the airport, check our bags, and get in the security line. The line isn't too long, and Dad says this is why he likes to fly at night. "We'll sleep on the plane and be ready for the day once we land on the East Coast," he tells me. We get through security and sit down at our assigned gate. There are families seated with small children who are dressed in pajamas for the overnight trip. A few people are reading books, and some are watching videos on their phones. There's a man who is bent over in the seat using his backpack as a pillow.

Dad and I sit near the ticket counter. "So do you have your must-see list?" Dad asks.

"Yep. Times Square, Top of the Rock, Riverbank State Park, Brooklyn Bridge Park, 125th Street, the Apollo, a play on Broadway—"

"You know we're only going to be there for a week, right?" Dad laughs.

I smile. "There's more, actually," I tell him.

"More?"

"Well, I want to see your neighborhood, visit the places that were important to you when you lived there."

A voice speaks over the intercom, announcing that it is time to board the plane.

Dad stands. "Ready?" he asks.

"Ready."

We board and find our seats near the front because Dad upgraded to have more legroom so his long legs won't cramp up. We get settled, seat belts on, snacks in the pouch on the back of the seats in front of us so we don't have to keep opening the overhead bins to get our carry-ons. I take out the activity book Mom gave me just in case I can't sleep and want to do a crossword puzzle.

After the safety demonstration is given, we take off. The lights dim, and a few flickers of light beam over seats where people are reading. Dad puts his seat back and puts his headphones on so he can watch his favorite late-night talk show. I hate to bother him, but I really want to ask him a question. I tap his arm. He pulls out the right earbud. "Yes?"

"You didn't tell me what you're looking forward to. Do

you have a must-see list?" I whisper because the woman across from us has an eye mask on and looks like she is already sleeping.

Dad says, "Well, no, I haven't really thought about that. I've just been focusing on what I need to do for work. And I want to make sure you have a good time."

"But there has to be something you want to do or someone you really want to see," I say. "Like, what's something we can't do in Oregon that we can do in New York?"

Dad thinks for a moment. "Get a Jamaican beef patty. Yeah, we have to do that. It will change your life. I promise you." Dad smiles just thinking about it. "I'll have to take you to the Concourse Jamaican Bakery in the Bronx. Best patties in New York City." Dad reaches for his earbud, and just before he puts it back in, he says, "And I have to take you to Canal Street and teach you how to haggle for good deals. You'll like that. We can get some souvenirs for your friends." For the first time Dad looks excited about this trip. "Get some sleep," he says. "Tomorrow's going to be a long day."

I put my headphones on, but I am not really paying attention to the screen. I can't stop thinking about all the things Dad and I will do in New York. I can't stop wondering what it's going to be like for Dad and Grandpa Earl to see each other for the first time in twelve years. How am I going to get them to talk to each other?

In all the ways I am like Dad, this is not one of them. There is no way I could ever, ever stop talking to him or Mom. I can't imagine it. I have been mad enough to stop talking to them for an hour, a night, but never whole weeks and months and years.

I really hope I don't make things worse. I mean, what if I get there and Grandpa Earl isn't happy at all to see me? Because I will just be a reminder that the day I was born his wife died. And the day I was born he stopped talking with his son. This might not be a good idea at all. Talking with Grandpa Earl on the phone is one thing, but maybe in person, things will be different. Maybe he will see me and only be reminded of the worst day of his life. I hope Mom is right about this being a good thing for me, for Dad, for Grandpa Earl.

I look out the window at the night sky. The tiny lights twinkle and glow below. I know they aren't stars, but I make a wish anyway.

9

When we get off the plane in New York, the first thing I do is call Mom. "How was the flight?" she asks.

"Good. We slept most of the way."

"Okay, well, tell your grandpa and everyone else that I said hello."

"Okay, Mom. Love you."

"Love you, too, Amara. Let me talk with your dad."

I give the phone to Dad, and he says a lot of "uh-huhs" and "yes, got its," as we follow the signs to baggage claim. Of all the things Mom told me about New York, she didn't tell me that JFK is huge compared to Portland's airport.

And the people. She didn't tell me that there would be so many people coming and going, going and coming. She didn't tell me I'd hear five languages in this one place.

After we get our luggage, we go outside to stand in the taxi line. It winds and twists and is just about as long as the lines at the Employee Store. The cold morning air stings my nostrils and chills my insides. I reach in my bag for my gloves. "Now you see what your mom was talking about, huh?" Dad asks. His breath zigzags in the air, making designs that quickly fade to nothing.

I nod and lean into him, resting my head on his chest. He puts his arms around me, and I get just a little warmer, but then the line moves so we separate. Even though my fingers are freezing, I take out my phone so I can take a picture of the line of taxis. The long trail of yellow cabs bends around the curve. I can't see where the line ends. "My first photo in New York," I say. Dad smiles. We get into the next cab, and for the first five minutes we zip along the freeway, making our way to Harlem, but then the car slows down to a stop and we sit and sit and inch our way through traffic for the next forty minutes. The constant jerking makes my stomach flip. "Dad, I don't feel good." It's colder than cold outside, but all of a sudden I feel hot. I unbutton my coat.

"You might be getting carsick," Dad says. Then he leans forward and says, "Easy on the brakes, please. I've got sensitive cargo back here."

The driver doesn't say anything.

I lean my head against Dad, think I'll just close my eyes for a little bit. I can't believe I've been in New York less than an hour and I'm sick.

"It'll pass," Dad says. He tells me to take deep breaths. I do, and it must calm me because the next thing I know Dad is shaking me and saying, "Amara, wake up. Amara, we're here."

I jump up. "We're here? I missed the drive?"

Dad pays for the ride, and we get out of the car. Dad was right—just standing up and being on solid ground makes me feel better. Better, not good. We stand outside Grandpa's brownstone. Dad doesn't walk up the steps yet; he just stands here taking it all in. He looks around at the street, and I wonder what memories are coming back, what memories he's pushing away.

All the brownstones look connected like one long

building with many doors. They stand tall like a box of crayons, except all the crayons are shades of brown. The tree-lined sidewalk is narrow, and the street is stuffed with cars parked bumper-to-bumper.

"Well, this is where I grew up," Dad says. "Many good times were had on this stoop." He breathes in, out.

Grandpa's home has a small garden behind an iron gate to the left side, where there's a small table and two chairs. We stand there, just looking at the house. I try to imagine Dad as a little boy running up and down these massive stairs, sitting out here on hot summer days, shoveling snow off them in the winter. Dad says, "Let's go in," and starts walking up the stairs. I follow him. I think maybe I should ask him if he's okay, but before I can come up with something to say and before we even make it all the way up the steps, the door opens. I don't know why but I take Dad's hand. An elderly man walks out, making his way down the steps. Grandpa Earl. He looks like the man in all the photos I've seen but older, more handsome, even. More real. He is real and walking toward me. I squeeze Dad's hand, and he holds on tight to mine. I think he might be just as nervous as I am. I hear him take a deep breath.

"Well, hello," Grandpa Earl says. Seeing him is like having a character from a movie or book come to life. He is here. Not just a smile in a photo, a voice on the phone. "Amara, you look just like my Grace. Just like her," he says. He reaches out to hug me. Being in his arms feels like trying on a thick winter coat that fits just right. I ease up a bit. He is hugging me, so maybe he is not upset with me, maybe he wants me here. Grandpa Earl looks at Dad, says, "Son."

Dad nods and takes our luggage into the house. Once we're all inside, I realize how big Grandpa's house is. On the outside it seems narrow, but once we walk through the door, I see that the first floor is wide and long and there's a staircase leading upstairs and another one at the back of the room, leading downstairs. Grandpa Earl says, "So how's my granddaughter doing?"

"Good," I say, because I am too embarrassed to say I feel like I might vomit, that the taxi ride here felt more like a roller coaster.

"Well, you make yourself at home, now, okay?" Grandpa Earl says. "I know you've had a long flight. Would you like breakfast?"

Dad doesn't answer.

I say, "Yes, please."

Grandpa Earl goes into the kitchen. "On a cold winter morning like this, you need something to warm your bones." He takes a canister down from on top of his fridge. The label on it says Oatmeal. I hate oatmeal, but I don't say anything. Grandpa Earl grabs the canister that says Brown Sugar on it, and he takes milk and butter out of the fridge. I've never seen someone actually make oatmeal. Mom uses those instant oatmeal packs on days when she doesn't feel like making breakfast, and she never puts sugar in it. Maybe I'll like it this way. "I figured I'd put you in your auntie's old room, Amara, and your dad can sleep in his old room. That all right with you . . . Charles?"

It isn't until this moment that we realize Dad isn't in here with us. He's already gone upstairs. I look at Grandpa Earl and tell him, "I'm sure it's fine." I go upstairs to find Dad. The second floor has a room in the front that's a smaller version of the living room downstairs. There are two armchairs and a small sofa that looks more like a cushioned bench. There are photos on the wall, so beautifully hung the room sort of feels like a museum. I stand in front of a photo of Dad and Grandma Grace. He must be five or six, and Grandma Grace has her arms wrapped around him like she is giving him all the love he'll ever need.

Looking at all these photos of Grandma Grace makes me wish she were here. I think maybe if she were still alive, Dad and Grandpa Earl would be talking and maybe we would have come to New York already and they would have come to Oregon to visit me. Maybe she would tell me about our family, our history. I wonder what it would be like to have a grandma who was not past tense but alive at the stove cooking breakfast, humming her favorite song, hugging me with all that love. I think of all my friends who have grandmas who sneak them candy when their parents aren't looking, who let them spend the night and stay up late watching TV even when it's way past their bedtime. I wonder, Would Grandma Grace be that kind of grandmother? Would her house be the mecca for family gatherings, where all the cousins and aunts and uncles come together to have summer cookouts and Thanksgiving feasts?

Would she tell me stories about growing up in

Alabama? What stories would she share about living in Harlem? I wonder and wonder about Grandma Grace. I miss her even though I never met her. I love her even though I never knew her.

When I get to Dad's room, I step inside, close the door, and whisper, "You're not being very nice to him."

"Amara, breakfast is going to get cold. Cold oatmeal is the nastiest thing in the world," Dad says.

"*Dad.*"

"Come on. Let's eat."

We walk back downstairs.

I keep thinking about what Mom asked me to do. I whisper a prayer to Grandma Grace, ask her to help me.

10

After breakfast, Grandpa Earl says, "Would you like to come with me for my Sunday morning walk? I usually stop by Lenox Coffee and shoot the breeze for a while."

"Sure," I tell him.

Grandpa puts on a navy blue coat and a brown fedora. He slides his gloves on.

I walk over to the closet and get my coat. "Dad, are you coming?"

"Oh, ah—you two can go ahead."

"Dad, you love coffee. You should come."

Grandpa says, "You'll barely recognize the block,

Charles. Lots of things have changed since you've been here."

I hand Dad his coat, not giving him a chance to say no. He puts it on slowly, like he is thinking of an excuse not to come, but I guess he can't think of one because he starts to button his coat and heads out the door.

As soon as the door opens, the cold air suffocates me. I take a deep breath, put my hands in my pocket. Grandpa and I walk side by side. Dad trails in back of us. Close enough that he can hear what we're saying but he is quiet and doesn't add anything to the conversation. At least he's here, walking with us.

"I'm glad it's dry," Grandpa says. "I was hoping the snow would hold off until after you and your father left."

"Really? I love snow," I tell Grandpa. "It doesn't snow a lot where I live. Well, it does in some parts, like at Mount Hood, but not a whole lot in the city. And when it does it's mostly the kind of snow that turns into ice, so we don't really get to be out in it."

"Well, we definitely get our fair share here," Grandpa Earl says. "It's beautiful to look at from the inside, but it's not so great when you have to be out in it. But maybe that's just the southerner in me talking."

"But you've lived in New York for a long time."

"Yeah, but Alabama is in my blood. I never did adjust to northern winters. But your grandma Grace? She loved snow. Winter was her favorite season."

I look back at Dad, ask him, "Did you like having snowy winters?"

"Well, as a boy—yes. Snow meant I got to play outside and have snowball fights with the kids on the block. But once I was old enough to shovel, snow meant getting out of bed early to clear off the stoop and sidewalk."

This is a start. Dad and Grandpa Earl are talking. Not to each other yet, but they are walking and talking with me, and that's good for day one.

We reach the end of the block, and even though the sign says Don't Walk, Grandpa looks down the one-way street and crosses anyway. When we get across the street, two men are walking and holding hands, and there's not enough room on the sidewalk for all of us to walk side by side, so Grandpa steps over to the right, I walk behind him, and once the men pass us we go back to walking together.

I wonder if Grandpa Earl and Grandma Grace ever walked this way on a morning walk. What were her favorite Harlem places? "What else did Grandma Grace like?" I ask.

Grandpa's face is the bright sun. "Oh, she liked a lot of things. She loved to garden, she enjoyed traveling. And she spent a lot of time reading. My Grace always had a book with her."

I love how Grandpa calls Grandma "my Grace," like she is his favorite everything.

We continue down the block, walking under leafless trees. The branches canopy over us. Cars honk their way down the street and come to a stop because a taxi is letting someone out of the car without pulling all the way over to the curb. A man yells out of the window, "Come on now!" He presses on his horn, and the cars behind him start honking, too, and now there is a symphony of beeping horns.

Grandpa keeps walking. "Here we are," he says as he opens the door to the coffee shop. Lenox Coffee is small with square wooden tables lined up so close to each other it seems impossible for anyone to walk between the aisles to find a seat.

As soon as we walk in, the man at the counter says, "Mr. Baker! How's it going?"

"Fine, just fine. Brought my granddaughter and son with me today." He smiles and puts his arm around me. "All the way from Or-e-gone," he says, mispronouncing Oregon.

The brown man whispers, "Oregon? There are black people out that way?"

Grandpa laughs. "I reckon we're everywhere, but some places more than others, that's for sure." Grandpa walks over to the bar at the counter to a seat that looks like it's been saved just for him. He hangs his coat on a nearby coatrack. Dad and I do the same. When Grandpa sits down at the bar, a steaming hot mug of coffee is already waiting for him. "Thank you," he says. "And a hot chocolate for her." He looks at Dad. "Charles, it's on me. What are you having?"

Dad orders but pays anyway. "I got it," he says to the cashier.

I hop up onto the stool next to Grandpa. Dad stands because no more seats are available.

I look around the coffee shop. There are so many shades of brown here. I've never seen this many black people in one room except at church. This place feels like some kind of church the way Grandpa says, "I know that's right, brotha," to the man working behind the counter. They are talking about politics. The two of them talk loud, as if there's no one else around, and maybe that's okay since everyone sitting at the too-small tables have headphones plugged in their ears anyway. Most of them are typing on laptops or reading thick books, marking pages with highlighters. There are a few people talking, but not many.

Grandpa Earl turns his attention to me and asks, "What do you want to do while you're here? Do you have a list?"

I smile at Dad. "Oh, yeah, I have a list." I tell Grandpa Earl everything on my list, and halfway through a tall man approaches Dad. There is shock and joy in the man's face all at once. He hugs Dad. Tight. I've only seen Dad give hugs like this to Big T.

"Charles Baker in the flesh. Man, why you didn't tell me you were in town?"

"Quick visit. Just here for a week," Dad says. "Mostly for work."

The man turns to Grandpa Earl. "Coach Baker, how you doin'?" He holds his hand out like he is going to shake

Grandpa Earl's hand, then pulls him in for a hug. When they let go of each other, the man says, "I'm still hoping you'll change your mind about joining us next season as assistant coach for my community league for teens. We could really use your expertise."

Grandpa Earl shakes his head. "Now I done told you I'm too old for that now. I retired many moons ago, and I am enjoying every minute." Grandpa Earl puts his hat on. "Plus, I coached you so you should know how to coach them." He pats the man on his shoulder.

The man nods. "I hear you, I hear you. A man can dream though."

Dad puts his arm around me and says, "Sorry to be rude. This is Amara, my daughter. Amara, this is Arnold Fuller. You can call him Mr. Arnold. We went to high school together."

"This is your daughter? Oh my—wow, how old are you now?"

"Almost twelve," I answer.

Mr. Arnold shakes my hand. "It's so nice to meet you. You look just like your dad, you know?"

I smile. Yeah, I know.

Mr. Arnold says to Dad, "Man, I haven't talked to you in forever. You still writing poems?"

Still?

Before Dad can answer, Mr. Arnold says, "Your dad sure had a way with words. He was like our school's in-house Shakespeare. I swore he was going to become some famous poet one day."

"*My* dad?"

Mr. Arnold laughs.

Dad lets out a long sigh, like he is tired of this conversation even though it just started.

"Yes, *your* dad. I was busy leading our basketball team to the city championship, and your dad was crushing on the poetry slam team."

I look at Dad, who looks like he's been caught doing something he shouldn't have.

Grandpa Earl says, "We're having family dinner at my place tonight, Arnold. You're welcome to come."

Dad says, "Yeah, come through and bring your wife. It's been too long."

"I will, I definitely will." He takes another look at Dad. "Man—Charles Baker. Can't believe this." Mr. Arnold gives us each another hug and walks to the barista to order.

Once Dad, Grandpa Earl, and I are finished with our drinks, we leave the coffee shop. There are so many questions swirling in my mind. We are halfway down the block when I finally break the silence and say, "Dad, I didn't know you wrote poems." Well, he mentioned something about it, but I thought he meant he wrote poems for Mom. Not that he was a poet.

Grandpa Earl says, "Yeah, your dad was always writing in a journal, always reading a book."

I turn and look at Dad. "I didn't know this about you."

Dad smiles. "Yeah, where do you think you get your love of reading from?"

When he says this I feel a soft pounding in my chest, like someone is knocking on my heart. The kind of knock a person gives when they know you are there but aren't sure if it's okay to come in. I start thinking about what Mom always says, wondering whose child I am. I think maybe I am not so different from Dad. We have more in common than just our love of shoes.

We stop at the corner and cross when the light changes. Grandpa says hello to every person he passes. At the corner one block away from Grandpa Earl's home, there's a gated playground. Even in this cold there are men outside playing basketball. Grandpa Earl says, "You remember this park, Charles?"

Dad nods.

Grandpa says to me, "We'd go to the park, and I'd try to get your dad to play basketball with the other boys, and he would for a little while, but before long, he was off wandering around the park or sitting under a tree with a pencil and notebook." Grandpa sounds sad when he says this. He sighs and says in a quiet, quiet voice, "I didn't understand him back then."

I look back at Dad, wonder if he heard Grandpa. Wonder if he is listening.

"What do you mean?" I ask Grandpa Earl, loud enough for Dad to hear me just in case he wants to join in on this conversation.

"Well, I guess I just didn't see a good reason why a boy would want to be writing in a journal all the time instead of being out with his friends. Charles just always had to have that notebook with him. And, well—" Grandpa Earl stops talking and just shakes his head. "I didn't understand him back then," he repeats.

I look back at Dad, and our eyes meet. Yeah, he's

listening. But he is giving me that look that lets me know I should not ask any more questions, that I need to drop it. So I do. For now.

We continue down the block, none of us saying a word. I whisper another prayer to Grandma Grace.

11

My first day in New York is ending with Sunday Supper. Aunt Tracey is here with her daughters. Nina and Ava are in high school. Nina is sixteen, Ava is fourteen. I have never met them in person, but Aunt Tracey always sends photos and I've talked to them on the phone a few times. Our conversations are always awkward because none of us can think of anything to talk about. I've seen Aunt Tracey a bunch of times when she's come to visit Oregon. She always says, "Next time I'll bring the girls," but she never does. Mom says it's because airfare is expensive and it costs too much for a family of three to travel when Aunt Tracey is the only one working.

Nina gives me a hug when she comes in. Ava does, too, but not as tight. She seems more interested in watching TV. She sits on the sofa, picks up the remote, and starts flipping through the channels. She does this like this is her home, like she is not a guest. I wonder how often she visits Grandpa Earl, wonder if this is her second home.

Dad comes downstairs and as soon as he enters the living room, Nina and Aunt Tracey are bombarding him with hugs. Ava gets up and hugs Dad, too. Dad looks them over. "It's so good to see all of you. Tracey, your girls aren't little girls anymore. My goodness."

Aunt Tracey smiles. "I feel the same way about Amara. Where did the time go?"

Grandpa Earl is sitting in an armchair, just watching and listening. He rubs his head and says, "My son and daughter and all my grandchildren in one place. How 'bout that."

I look at my family, study them for a moment. Nina and Ava look just like Aunt Tracey, who looks like Dad. Not just in features but the way they move, how their faces make the same expressions, have some of the same mannerisms. I wonder if my baby sister will look like me. Will

I see my reflection in her smile or hear echoes of my voice in her laughter?

"I better get dinner ready," Aunt Tracey says.

"I can help." I've always wanted to cook in Grandma Grace's kitchen.

"Well thank you, Amara." She looks at Nina and Ava, who are now watching *The Wiz* with Grandpa Earl. She shakes her head and says, "Come with me."

Aunt Tracey takes out a pot from one of the cabinets. It is deep and wide. She teaches me how to make gumbo, and we make corn bread, too. Once the corn bread is finished baking and has cooled a bit, Aunt Tracey says, "Slice the corn bread for me, baby." She shows me how before handing me the knife. "In square chunks like this."

The last dish Aunt Tracey is making is dessert. Banana pudding. Dad's favorite. Dad comes into the kitchen, looking into the pot and snooping around. Aunt Tracey shoos him away, swatting him with a hand towel.

"I can't get a taste test . . . a little sample? Just like Momma," Dad says.

They laugh, and Aunt Tracey says, "I'm not completely like her. You see I'm the only one in here working. I can't get

Nina and Ava to be interested one bit in cooking. Momma had us in the kitchen up under her all the time. But these girls? They'd rather be on their phones or glued to the TV."

Dad smiles. He looks at me, pulls me close, and says, "This one right here is my little sous chef. I'm trying to pass Momma's good cooking down to her."

It feels so good to be in his arms. To have him holding me while he's talking about Grandma Grace.

Ava comes into the kitchen. "Mom, you're in here cooking like it's a holiday."

"Well, it's a special occasion," Aunt Tracey says.

Ava looks at Dad. "You should come visit more often, Uncle Charles."

"Hush now," Aunt Tracey says, laughing.

Mr. Arnold and his wife arrive, with a few other friends that Dad hasn't seen in years. Everyone gets to hugging and laughing and fixing plates. We don't sit at the formal dining room table; instead we are scattered all over the living room and kitchen, fitting in wherever we can. The television is off now, and Grandpa Earl has a jazz record playing on his record player. I can barely hear the music because everyone is talking so loud.

Aunt Tracey, Mr. Arnold, and Dad have been telling stories about all the wild things they did when they were my age. Aunt Tracey says, "Remember that time we snuck in the church's kitchen and drank up all the grape juice during Sunday school so there wasn't any left once the deacons were ready to prepare Communion?"

Everyone laughs.

Nina says, "Mom, you would lose it if me and Ava did that."

"You got that right. Glad you know, so don't even try it."

We all laugh harder.

Aunt Tracey says, "I'm serious. I can't have you out there acting like you have no home training. You two represent the Baker family."

Dad mumbles, "You sound like your father right now. Worried about the Baker name."

Aunt Tracey gives him a Don't-Start-That look and keeps talking, like Dad didn't just say what we all heard him say. "So, Amara, tell me—what are you into these days? The last time I was in Oregon I could barely pull you away from your books."

Grandpa says, "Sounds like Charles."

When he says this, Dad puts his fork down. "And what's wrong with that?"

It's my turn to give Dad a look.

Grandpa Earl says, "Nothing wrong with it at all, son. Nothing at all."

Mr. Arnold is either clueless to the tension or trying to help. He says, "Do you write poetry, too, Amara? Maybe you'll be a poet just like your dad."

Dad gets up and goes into the kitchen. "Nah, I want Amara to be who she wants to be. I'm not trying to create a mini-me." He looks at Grandpa. "I don't want *my* child growing up with pressure to be someone she's not."

The room is quiet. It's not the kind of quiet that happens because everyone is eating and there's no time for words, not the quiet that comes at the end of the day with a good friend who you've talked and talked with for hours and have run out of things to say but you still want to be together. No, this silence is not refreshing or comforting. It feels stuffy like a too-hot attic, like the inside of a car that's been sitting in the hot sun all day.

Finally the silence breaks. "When are we going to get into this banana pudding?" Dad asks.

Nina and Ava go into the kitchen and help Dad dish out dessert.

I look at Grandpa Earl, try to tell him *sorry* with my eyes.

He smiles a little. Just a little.

Nina has two bowls in her hand. She gives one to me and then says to Grandpa Earl, "Are you having dessert?"

"No, thank you. I think I'm going to call it a night. This old man can't hang as late as all of you can." Grandpa Earl gets up, says good night to everyone, and goes to his room.

I feel my phone buzzing. It's Mom wanting to Face-Time. How did she know to call at this moment? I answer. "Hi, Mom."

"Hey, Amara. Wanted to talk with you before it gets too late. How's everything going?"

"Um, good. Things are—we just finished dinner. Things are good." I try to sound convincing, but I am not sure it's working.

Mr. Arnold comes behind me and says, "Hey, Leslie.

It's a blast from your past!" Mom screams, and I hand the phone over so they can talk. After Mr. Arnold and his wife talk with Mom, the phone passes like a Communion tray. Aunt Tracey talks with Mom next, then Nina and Ava share their turn. When they're finished, they give the phone to Dad.

Dad asks, "How's the baby?"

"Well, I had Braxton Hicks last night, so I'm just taking it easy today and resting."

"And you weren't going to tell me?"

"Honey, I'm calling now. I was going to fill you in. I know you're with your family. I don't want you to worry. I'm fine. I'm fine."

"I can come home now, Leslie. Just say the word."

"I'm fine," Mom says.

Aunt Tracey notices me listening to every word my parents are saying, so she taps Dad on his leg, says, "Maybe you should go upstairs."

Dad leaves, and I really want to follow him, want to hear everything Mom is saying about having Braxton Hicks, whatever that is. I want to listen to Mom's voice, see if there is any worry there, any fear.

Aunt Tracey comes over to me, says, "Don't worry. I had false contractions with Ava. It's normal. Your mom is okay and the baby will be healthy." Aunt Tracey scoots closer to me, and just having her next to me makes me feel better. A little.

I don't feel like eating my banana pudding, but I don't want to waste food, either. I eat a spoonful. Dad calls me upstairs. I take the phone, go into Aunt Tracey's room, and close the door. I look into Mom's face. The first thing she says to me is, "I'm okay. I'm fine."

"Promise?"

"Promise. The baby is okay," she says. "How's our secret challenge going?"

"Not good," I whisper. I tell Mom about dinner and about the walk home from the coffee shop. "This is going to be harder than I thought," I tell Mom.

She says, "If anyone can bring those two together, it's you."

12

The next morning Dad is out of the house before Grandpa Earl makes our oatmeal. He has a breakfast meeting and then a site visit at the NBA store. Grandpa Earl says, "I can call your cousins and see if they can take you out today. They're on midwinter break. I'm sure they need something to do." Grandpa Earl might be the only person I know who has a landline. He picks up his phone and dials the number from memory. He must have the volume as loud as it goes because I can hear every word they're saying and it doesn't sound good. "Grandpa, we don't feel like baby-sitting," Ava says.

"You're not babysitting, Ava. You're spending time with your cousin. She's here all the way from Oregon. Don't you want to get to know her?"

"We just hung out with her all night last night."

"I want you to come over and spend some time with her. Isn't your momma at work? You two don't need to be sitting up in the house by yourselves all day."

Nina must have grabbed the phone because now she is talking. "Grandpa, we'll be there as soon as we finish getting dressed."

Grandpa Earl hangs up the phone and then says, "They can't wait to show you around."

Does he really think I didn't hear them?

Within the hour, Nina and Ava are ringing the doorbell. They hug Grandpa Earl, and the way he lights up lets me know they are two of his favorite people. He doesn't look at me that way, but how can he? He doesn't know me.

"Hi, Amara," Nina says to me. Her hair is a whirlwind of curls. The thick black coils fall to her shoulders. Ava doesn't say anything; she walks straight to the kitchen and goes into the pantry, taking out a box of Nilla Wafers. They're both dressed like they're going somewhere special, not just sightseeing. Their faces are painted with makeup, and their clothes look like they were put together by a professional stylist.

Me on the other hand? I don't know the first thing about putting on makeup—not that Mom would let me wear it anyway. I'm wearing jeans and a T-shirt with the Nikes Titus gave me. And, of course, once we go outside I'll have on a hoodie under the winter coat Mom got just for this trip. Their coats are what Mom calls "cute but not practical."

Grandpa Earl walks over to the door and grabs a key off a hook that's hanging under a mirror. He tells Nina and Ava, "Here, take the spare key so you can let yourselves back in. And just stay near the house. Take her over there to 125th and let her see the Apollo."

"Grandpa, no one wants to see the Apollo," Ava says.

"Yes, I do," I admit.

Ava doesn't think I see her rolling her eyes. "What about going to Times Square or someplace like that?" she asks.

Grandpa Earl shakes his head. "Just stay close to home."

Grandpa gives Nina and Ava a lecture about looking out for me and making sure I have a good time. "We got it, Grandpa. We got it," Ava says. She mumbles to Nina, "Grandpa acts like we've never been nowhere before."

We walk outside. "Let's walk down to Lenox and then we can head over to 125th," Nina says.

We walk on 129th, and when we get to Lenox, we turn left. I look at the street sign and notice that it's also called Malcolm X Boulevard. "Can we stop so I can take a picture of the sign?"

"What sign?" Ava asks.

I point.

"You want a picture of that?" Ava looks all kinds of confused.

I take my phone out and zoom in so I am sure to get the full name. I take the picture and think how I will include this somehow in my suitcase. We make our way down Lenox Avenue. Every now and then Ava turns to me and says, "Stop looking like you don't belong here," but I don't know what she means by that so I just keep walking.

The streets aren't as crowded as I thought they would

be. The sidewalks are wide, and even with a few vendors on the edge of the sidewalks, there's still plenty of room to walk. I am thinking maybe Mom was exaggerating about how busy New York is, with its bustling streets, but then we get to the corner of 125th and Lenox. There's a crowd of people crossing the street going both directions and cars forging their way through and whizzing by. There's a Starbucks on the left and a subway station on the corner. I want to take a picture of the subway entrance, but I know Ava will think I'm making a big deal out of nothing, so I just act like it's not a big deal that there's an actual entryway to an underground tunnel. I wonder what it's like to be underground, to have a whole world moving above you. I think about the fact that we are walking on top of people who are moving around under us having a whole different experience than we are.

There is so much to look at, I don't know where to put my eyes. I look up at the street sign and see that 125th is also called Dr. Martin Luther King Jr. Boulevard. I wonder why streets here have one name and then another, like there are two worlds here, two ways to go. I want to get a picture of where Malcolm X and Dr. Martin Luther

King Jr. Boulevards intersect, but the light changes and we need to cross.

We turn right onto 125th. It is full of people, some moving quickly, some walking slow, others standing and watching it all. There are vendors set up on both sides of the street selling everything from purses to black art to incense and perfume, to jewelry, to gloves and scarves. A long line is in front of the cart across the street where people are waiting to buy a hot dog, pretzel, or roasted peanuts. I stop and pull out my phone so I can take a picture. A woman bumps into me, and Ava goes to fussing at me while Nina apologizes to the woman. "You can't just stop in the middle of the street," Ava says. "And what is there to take a picture of anyway?" she asks.

"Come on," Nina says. "We'll stop at the Apollo, and you can take a picture there. But other than that, we have to keep it moving."

The more we walk on 125th, the more people there are to navigate through. The sidewalks are too crowded for the three of us to walk side by side. Nina and I walk next to each other. Ava is in back of us. "Ooh—H&M. Let's stop in here," she says.

Nina shakes her head. "We are not shopping. We're supposed to be showing Amara around Harlem. She doesn't want to shop at H&M."

Nina is right.

Ava huffs and walks faster. "Well, can we at least go on the way back after she sees everything?"

"Yes," Nina says.

"Well, come on, then." Ava leads the way, and we follow. She is walking so fast and so far ahead she doesn't hear it when Nina says, "Let's stop here so she can see the statue." Nina has to call out to her twice to get her attention. We stop in front of a statue of a man with his coat jacket swaying in the imagined wind. He looks like he is moving, going somewhere and looking straight ahead with a determined face.

"Are we going to stop at every little thing?" Ava asks.

Nina gives her a look, and Ava gets quiet, and I think maybe later I will ask Nina how to give the Big-Sister-Stare-Down in case I'll need to use it on my baby sister one day.

Ava walks back and joins us in front of the statue. "This is Adam Clayton Powell," Nina says. "He was a politician and fought for—"

"He was a preacher," Ava cuts in. "That's what Grandpa told me."

"I think he was both," Nina says, not at all masking that she is irritated with her sister. "The point is, he did a lot for Harlem. He organized rent strikes and fought to integrate places of business so that black people could work anywhere and get fair pay."

I take a few pictures, then take a photo of the silver pillar he is standing on. There are words written on the side: Keep the Faith, it says. Sitting on the benches that wrap around the statue are groups of people eating and talking on their phones and blowing into their cold hands. Three drummers entertain a small group of people who've crowded around them. They tap and hit the African drums, their hands moving fast and dancing in the air. A few people have their phones out and are recording; others sway from side to side. And then there are people who walk by as if they don't hear the beat of the drum at all, as if it's normal to have an African drum session in the middle of the sidewalk.

I lift my arms up high and take a photo of the whole scene. "Nothing like this happens in Beaverton," I say.

Nina says, "Maybe we'll visit one day. My mom is always saying it's a shame she doesn't see her brother much."

"I'll show you around if you come," I tell them. And I won't be annoyed when they notice how instead of tall, tall buildings stretching to the sky there are pine trees standing tall like ladders you can climb into the clouds. And when they want the car to slow down so they can take out their cameras and capture Mount Hood towering over the city, looking close enough to touch, I'll understand. And every time they say, "It's just so clean here," I won't sigh or huff and puff. I know I can promise this because this is what Titus said when he first moved to Oregon, and I never—not once—made him feel bad for noticing how different our worlds were.

We keep walking, and then I see marquee of the Apollo just ahead of us. I try to act like it's no big deal, especially since Nina and Ava don't seem to care at all. Once we're standing under it, I realize there are other people out here taking photos, so at least I'm not the only one. "Have you ever been inside?" I ask.

"A bunch of times," Ava says.

I can hardly hear her because there's a man not too far away speaking into a megaphone about Jesus being the white man's god, and not too far from him, there's a man yelling out, "Got your gloves right here, right here. Got scarves, got hats. Cold out here. Got your gloves right here."

I take a few pictures of the marquee, and all I can think about is all the stories I've heard about Michael Jackson and James Brown singing at the Apollo, how performers would rub the wooden stump for good luck.

I swipe through all the photos I've taken so far, choosing one to send to Titus. Titus replies to my text with a photo of his math book and a message that says, Nothing exciting happening here.

Nina looks at my phone. "Who's that?" she asks.

"My best friend, Titus."

"Your best friend is a *boy*?" Ava sings. "Does your mom know you have a boyfriend?"

"No, he's not my boyfriend. He's my best friend."

"Mmm-hmm, okay," Nina says.

I put my phone in my pocket.

"Come on, let's go down Frederick Douglass." Nina

leads the way and once we are at the corner, I see the two street signs at the top of the pole. Dr. Martin Luther King Jr. Boulevard and Frederick Douglass Boulevard. I stop to take another picture. I say to Nina and Ava, "Can you imagine what it would be like if Frederick Douglass really met Martin Luther King on a corner? I wonder what they would say to each other?"

Nina says, "That's a good question."

And I think maybe Nina has an answer to give, but Ava interrupts, shrugging her shoulders and saying, "Let's turn here. You'll probably like this street."

We turn left onto Frederick Douglass, and Ava was right. I do love it. There are restaurants and stores block after block, and then I see a statue of Harriet Tubman in the middle of the street, in its own sectioned-off space. Like Adam Clayton Powell, she looks like she is in motion, looks like she is running. I don't even have to ask to stop to take a photo. Nina and Ava cross the street, and we stand at the statue taking it all in. Now that I am closer, I see roots are coming from her back, digging into the ground.

I take pictures. "I think I'll print these and put them in my suitcase," I say. I tell them about the Suitcase Project, and Ava says, "Oh, so that's why you're taking pictures of everything," like my homework assignment is the only reason why I want to capture the place where my dad was born, the place that raised him. I take a few of the whole statue, making sure I get some close-ups. First, the face. She is not smiling, but she doesn't look angry. She looks determined, courageous. I walk around her, look at the back of the statue. There are footprints stamped around the bell of her dress, and faces carved in the bronze. I take close-ups of the faces and footprints, think about how many people she led to freedom. Then there are the roots. They are brown and thick and intertwined with each other, anchoring the statue into the cement. I take a picture of the roots, get real close.

Ava reaches for my phone and says, "You want to get in one of the photos so you can send it to your boyfriend?" She smiles when she says this, and Nina laughs, but I don't think it's funny, and even though I do want to be in the picture, I don't want her to take it. I give my phone to Nina and say, "Let's take a selfie." We pose in front of Harriet Tubman, and I am starting to understand why Big T is always saying there's no place like New York. No place else that constantly reminds us that we are important, that we come from a people who sacrificed and fought and protested for us to be able to walk these streets free. What is it like to be reminded of this every day?

In Oregon, I only see stuff like this in museums when there's a special exhibit up that celebrates black history. But here—right outside in the middle of street—there's a reminder. I wonder if the people who live here ever stop to take it in. Do they ever stand here, say a prayer of thanksgiving?

"Can we please walk back now?" Ava says. "I just want to look in H&M for a little bit. I promise I won't take long."

We head back to 125th Street toward the store. The whole time I'm walking, I am thinking about those statues. Adam Clayton Powell and Harriet Tubman in motion. Eyes fixed on something far, far away. Feet rooted and grounded.

I want to feel like that. Like I am connected to something, like there's a history keeping me moving, living. Like the journey I am on has many footprints, many stories coming with me.

We spend an hour in the store because Ava is trying on outfits and can't make up her mind about what she wants. "Why aren't you trying anything on?" she asks.

I shrug as if I don't have an answer. I wish I had the boldness to tell her that I did not come all the way to New York to shop at a store that I can shop at in Oregon. Ava tries on another dress, then after talking with the woman at the counter she says, "Let's go to the one in Times Square. They're holding this in my size." She holds up a hunter green dress.

I look at Nina. "But Grandpa Earl said—"

Before I can finish my sentence, Ava tells me, "Grandpa is probably taking a nap. He won't even know that you're still gone."

Nina is quiet and then says, "Okay, but we're only going to H&M, and then we're back on the train."

We walk out of the store back onto the crowded street and make our way to the subway. To my left a woman stands begging for money. A few people drop coins in her paper cup. When we get underground, Nina says, "We need to get you a MetroCard." She walks over to the vending machine. "Wait right here."

I stand with Ava, who doesn't seem to notice the man pop-locking just a few steps away from her. The music is only in his head, and he's dancing hard like he's on a stage performing. Part of me wants to laugh, but I also feel sadness for him. Two kids go under the turnstile, not paying their fare. I see an elderly woman watching them, shaking her head.

Nina walks over to us and hands me a thin plastic card. "Don't lose this," she says. She shows me how to swipe it, and the first time I do it too fast, so when I try to walk through the turnstile, the metal pole hits my leg, doesn't let me in. I try it again, slower this time, and walk through. When we get on the platform the first thing I notice is that there are rats running along the tracks. Not mice. Big, fat rats. Even though they are below us, nowhere near me at all, I step back farther from the edge and try not to look at them. Nina notices and laughs at me. "They don't have rodents in Oregon?" she asks. "Come on, let's walk down so we can be at the back of the train."

We make our way to the end of the platform. The tiled walls have colorful mosaics of black activists, musicians, and artists flying through the sky. I take a few photos.

I say to Nina and Ava, "For my project, I have to interview family members. Can I interview you?" I don't have Mr. Rosen's questions with me, but I already know what I want to ask, already know I don't need to write down their answers. I'll never forget anything about this trip.

Nina and Ava say I can ask them anything. I begin, "So what is it like living here?"

"I don't know," Ava says. "It's like this." She points out at the crowd on the platform. There's a woman walking down the concrete stairs carrying a stroller. The baby inside is bobbling up and down as its mother makes her way to the platform. A man wearing something that looks like a dress, but is not a dress, runs over to help her. "What is it like in Oregon?" Ava asks.

And all I can think to say is, "It's not like this."

Now all of a sudden they are interviewing me. Nina asks, "Where else have you been?"

"LA twice, Seattle a bunch of times, and Atlanta once," I tell them.

Ava's eyes bulge out like she's witnessing the biggest surprise. "Really?"

"Sometimes my mom and I get to travel with my dad

for work. But this is the first time I've ever come on a trip without Mom," I tell them. "Our first daddy-daughter trip."

"I'm so jealous," Nina says, and I don't know if she's jealous because she doesn't travel as much as me or because she doesn't have a father like I do. Well, technically she has a father—everyone does, I guess. But Nina and Ava's dad is in jail. And this is something else Mom and Dad never really talk about. I want to ask Nina and Ava about their dad, but as soon as I come up with a question to ask, Nina asks me, "You always wear your hair like that?"

"In a ponytail?" I ask.

"Straight," she answers. "Do you ever wear it natural?"

"It is natural."

Ava jumps in. "Your hair is not naturally straight. You have a perm, right?"

"No. I've never had chemicals in my hair. It's natural. I just flat iron it." I have never had black girls ask about my hair. Only the white girls I go to school with, especially when it's braided.

Ava is all, "You can't say your hair is natural if it didn't grow out of your head like that."

Nina nudges her. Hard.

"What? Her hair isn't natural," Ava repeats.

"And yours is?" I ask, not to be smart with her but because now I am confused and I really want to know. "You must put something in your hair to get it curly like that."

"No. I mean, well, yes," Ava says. "I oil it and keep it moisturized. And I twist it to give it some style, but I am not *changing* the actual texture of my hair."

She says this like she wants some kind of prize.

"Oh, well, my mom straightens it because she says it's easier to manage this way."

Ava sucks her teeth, rolls her eyes, and puts her headphones on like she can't bear to be a part of this conversation. She steps forward and looks to the left to see if a train is coming. Nothing.

Nina says, "I only asked because I really like it. And my mom won't let us straighten our hair."

"Never?"

"She says when we're out of her house we can do whatever we want with it," Nina tells me. "I'll probably cut it once I graduate."

The subway train bolts into the station, bringing a cold breeze with it. "Stay close to me," Nina says as she forges her way through the open doors. It is so crowded I can't help but bump up against the other passengers. Our thick coats rub each other, and there are hands on top of hands all over the silver poles in the middle of the aisle, so many that when Ava tells me to hold on, I can barely find an empty spot.

The train chugs along, and I try to keep my balance. When we jerk to a stop, I stumble into the person next to me. He smiles and moves over just a little. People move in and out, and we all shift. Nina is now closer to the sliding doors, and I'm still holding on to the pole. Ava found a seat—well, kind of. She's squished between two people with hardly enough space to scoot all the way back. When we get to the next stop, a woman gets on with a violin. She starts to play it, only instead of classical music, which I expect, she's playing something with a hip-hop beat and she's singing and rapping. She plays for two stops, and then goes to the next car. At the next stop, there's another shifting and I move farther away from where Ava and Nina are. Nina mouths, *Get off in two more stops.*

We pass Ninety-Sixth Street, then Seventy-Second.

The automated voice announces that we are at Times Square. When the doors open people push in and out and I almost don't make it off before the doors start to close. A man sways his backpack over the threshold of the door to keep it open. "Thank you," I say.

I get off the subway and step onto the platform. The platform is full, and I don't see Nina or Ava anymore. All the dark winter coats look the same, and the sea of people blend together. I feel sick, and not the car sickness I had when I first got here, but the Oh-My-God-I'm-Lost-in-New-York sick. The We-Disobeyed-Grandpa-Earl-and-Now-Look-What-Happened kind of sick.

I stand alone in the middle of the platform, looking side to side.

There are two boys banging buckets like drums, making beats and entertaining the crowd. It's so loud, I can barely hear the automated voice making announcements. Another train on the other side of the platform pulls in and screeches to a stop. Somehow, through all this noise, I hear Ava's voice calling out my name. And when I see her and Nina, I could cry. Ava says, "Why you standing there looking like that? Come on." She walks up the stairs.

Nina tells Ava, "Slow down." She looks at me. "Walk in the middle of us. Keep up." Nina walks behind me, and I feel better knowing that her eyes are on me.

Ava is walking fast, and I think to myself how I am going to ask Mom why she didn't say anything about all these stairs you have to climb in New York City. I'm out of breath when we reach the top, but Ava keeps going. Then, finally, there's an escalator, so we ride up to the ground level, and when we step outside the subway station, I gasp. "Now I feel like I'm in New York," I say.

Ava rolls her eyes, and Nina nudges her and whispers, "Be nice."

I try to see every single detail of Times Square. The oversized television screens suspended in the sky and on the sides of buildings. Buildings so high you feel how ants must feel—tiny and easily destructible. Walking through the streets, I see lights shining around the marquees of Broadway theaters and street artists sketching portraits of tourists.

"Give me your phone," Ava says to me. She knows I want a picture. She takes a few of me with a lit-up Times Square in the background, and then I take some of just the signs and people.

Nina says, "Okay, put that in your purse, not your pocket, and don't take it back out. Don't stare up, either. Just act like you live here."

That's going to be impossible.

I put my phone away, and we walk to H&M. As we walk, Nina says, "Ava, I mean it—go in, try on the dress, leave it or buy it, and then we have to go. No looking around."

"Okay, okay."

"Is Grandpa Earl going to be mad when he finds out where we went?" I ask.

Ava says, "He's not going to find out. But even if he did, he wouldn't be too mad. He'd fuss for a bit, but that's all. He's not as strict as our mom."

"Oh."

"Is your dad strict?" Ava asks.

"Not really," I answer.

"I didn't think so," Nina says. "Uncle Charles seems real chill."

Hearing them call my dad "Uncle Charles" makes me wish I had cousins around me all the time. That I knew what it was like to walk around town having people point to me, telling me I look just like so-and-so or asking me if I'm related to the Baker family.

"What about your dad? I mean, is he . . . was he—"

"We don't have many memories of our dad," Nina says, speaking for both of them. "Our dad left when we were four and two, so, you know, we were too young to know him enough to really remember him."

I notice Nina says "left," not "went to jail."

I notice Ava, for once, says nothing.

Nina tells me, "Grandpa is kind of like our dad. He helped our mom raise us. We're really close."

Now I am feeling jealous, but I know that I shouldn't. I have a dad and I see him every day. Why do I care if they are closer to Grandpa Earl than I am?

Nina rushes Ava to go get the dress and try it on so we can get back to Harlem. We stand and wait for her, looking through a basket of rings. We test them out, trying them on and swapping them with one another. I guess my asking about Nina's father got her thinking about him because she starts talking about him again even though I haven't asked another question. "My dad writes us twice a month," she tells me. "And we write him back." Nina wiggles a ring off her pointer finger. It is tight, so she has to turn and twist it a few times before it comes off. "When I turn eighteen, I'm going to go visit him. Mom thinks we're too young to see him behind glass. But once I graduate, I am going."

Nina says this like it's a declaration.

"Two more years. Just two more," she says.

I imagine Nina, eighteen years old, with her newly cut hair, making a trip to visit her dad. And I think how even though she has Grandpa Earl, she still wants her dad, too. I guess maybe we all want to be connected to our roots.

13

I know my birthday isn't here yet and I have no candle to blow out, but as soon as I wake up, I make a wish, say a prayer. *God, please let my baby sister be okay.* And then I say a prayer asking that I get some interviews done today. It's Tuesday, and so far I only have bits and pieces, not enough to complete my assignment. I've got to finish talking with Nina and Ava and stay focused next time so that I am the only one asking questions. And Grandpa Earl. I've got to interview him, too.

I ease out of bed, take my time getting dressed, and go downstairs. Grandpa is in the kitchen already, making oatmeal. "I was just about to call up to you," he says. "Good morning."

"Good morning."

"Hungry?" he asks, pointing to the sliced apples sitting on a plate.

"Thank you," I say, biting into the sweet fruit. "Is Dad up yet?"

"He's got meetings all day. Left about ten minutes ago."

I don't say anything. Just stuff my mouth with more apple.

"But don't you fret. The girls will be here soon, and I've planned a little outing. There are some places I want to show you that aren't on your list," Grandpa Earl says. "Hope you don't mind spending the day with an old man."

"Not at all," I say.

After breakfast, I wash the dishes and clean up the kitchen. Grandpa Earl disappears into his bedroom to get dressed. I stand in the living room looking around, wondering what stories this brownstone holds. There's an oak cabinet across from me pushed against the wall. It looks like an antique thing, something Mom would use as a prop in a photo shoot of her vintage wedding gowns. On top of it are black-and-white photos of Grandma Grace and the rest of the family over the years. I wonder what's inside. I walk over to open the doors, hoping to get a quick peek before Grandpa Earl returns, but then the doorbell rings.

Nina and Ava are here, dressed to impress again.

Grandpa comes out of his room, grabs his coat and keys, and we leave.

Because we're with Grandpa Earl, we are walking slowly and I can actually look around without feeling rushed by Ava. We walk by a restaurant on 126th and Lenox that has a mural. "Can we stop? I want to take a picture," I say.

Ava doesn't roll her eyes this time. Maybe because Grandpa Earl is with us, maybe because she doesn't want to get that Big-Sister-Stare-Down from Nina again.

Grandpa Earl says, "I wanted you to see this." We all step close to the mural. A Harlem neighborhood is painted against the brick. Black legends float through the air, some smiling, some holding hands, others reaching into the sky as if they are offering up a praise or flying away to heaven.

Grandpa takes out his wallet. "I'll give you each a dollar for every person you recognize."

Ava is quick to shout out, "Madam C. J. Walker," then

looks at me, rolls her eyes, and says, "She invented the process for *straightening* hair."

I really don't understand why she has an attitude about me straightening my hair.

I point and say, "Michael Jackson!"

Then Nina says, "Maya Angelou . . . President Barack Obama."

And at the same time Nina and I call out, "Adam Clayton Powell!" He is in a blue suit flying through the air, one hand in a fist, the other open and stretched out, looking like some kind of superhero.

Grandpa opens his wallet and gives us single dollar bills as we call out names. Ava says, "That's Josephine Baker, right?"

Grandpa nods and gives her a dollar.

I scan the wall. "Ooh, ooh, there's Malcolm X!"

Grandpa hands me another dollar and says, "All right, looks like I'm all out of cash." There are so many people on the wall that we haven't said yet. Grandpa tells us, "I'm glad you recognized so many. It's important to know the ones who've come before us, who we're connected to."

Before we leave, I take my camera, zoom in, take more photos.

We continue on Lenox, toward 135th Street. Fewer people are on the sidewalks, and there aren't as many street vendors this way, except for one man who is selling hats, gloves, and all types of scarves.

"Here we are," Grandpa says when we get to 135th. "This is the Schomburg Center. This is a haven for black history."

We wait to cross the street, and then, when no traffic is coming, we all walk into the street even though the light hasn't changed. When we step inside, Grandpa says hello to the man sitting behind the front desk. "Earl, my man, good to see you," the man says, and reaches to shake Grandpa's hand.

I think Grandpa Earl must know everyone in Harlem.

Grandpa Earl introduces me to his friend and then says, "Go 'head and give her the spiel. Act like we've never heard it before."

"Well, all right," the man says.

Ava sighs, and this makes me think that maybe Grandpa Earl has brought her here before, that she already knows everything this man is about to say.

The man stands, handing all three of us girls a brochure. "We're a research library, which means you can't

119

check out any books. But many people come here to do in-depth research on black culture. We have all sorts of materials about the African American, African diaspora, and African experiences—"

Grandpa Earl interrupts. "People can come here to look through the writings, photos, and keepsakes from African American legends."

Nina whispers to me and Ava, "Grandpa might as well work here."

Grandpa Earl keeps going: "The man it's named after, Arturo Alfonso Schomburg, was a young boy in school when one of his teachers told him that black people had no history, that we hadn't accomplished anything important. Mr. Schomburg wanted to prove his teacher wrong, and he searched to find out what we, as a people, had contributed to the world."

The man at the desk adds on, "He was a Puerto Rican of African and German descent. He dedicated his life to researching and raising awareness of the achievements of Afro-Latin Americans and African Americans."

Grandpa Earl interrupts again, asking, "Isn't it his collection of literature, art, and slave narratives that started this whole research center?"

"You know your history, Earl," the man says.

Grandpa Earl turns to us and says, "This place was created with you in mind." I know he is talking to all three of us, but for some reason, I feel like he is especially talking to me. Our eyes meet when he says, "Your ancestors wanted to preserve your history, wanted there to be a place where you could come and hold on to your roots, know the story of how you got here."

Finally, the man behind the desk speaks again. "They may not have known you by name, but they had you in mind."

Grandpa Earl shakes the man's hand again and says, "Let's go inside."

We walk through the lobby and enter a separate room. The floor is covered with mosaic tile. Grandpa Earl tells us, "This cosmogram is a tribute to Schomburg and the poet Langston Hughes." He points to the words engraved on the floor. "Langston's poem, 'The Negro Speaks of Rivers,' was his first critically acclaimed poem, and this installation honors his life and the diaspora. His ashes are buried underneath."

"His ashes?" I say, a little too loud, because a woman walking by looks at me with the sternest eyes.

"Yes, this is a sacred place," Grandpa Earl says. "I'll leave you here so you can take it all in. When you're finished here, go on upstairs to see the exhibit on James Baldwin."

Ava says, "But, Grandpa, I've already seen all of this. My school came on a field trip."

"Look again. There's always more to see." He walks away, leaving me, Nina, and Ava standing in the middle of the cosmogram.

Ava tells us that she is going to the gift shop, and Nina says, "I'll be upstairs," and walks away, so now I am alone. I step into the center, place my feet right at the tip of the words to his poem: *My soul has grown deep like the rivers.* I don't take my phone out to capture this. I just want to stand here, just want to be.

People walk by, coming and going. The elevator dings, voices echo, footsteps tap against the tile. But I don't move. I breathe in this place, think of all the activists and artists, politicians and preachers and teachers who've walked in here, think how Grandpa Earl said this was created with me in mind.

I wonder if my ancestors saw me coming. How far into

the future could they imagine? Just the idea that people like Harriet Tubman, Adam Clayton Powell, and Langston Hughes were thinking that one day someone like me would exist in a free world makes my heart pound, my eyes water.

I study the cosmogram, which looks like a map to me. Like a blueprint of all the places black people have been, all the places we bring with us, all the rivers and stories that come with us. The Euphrates, the Nile, the Mississippi.

I think about Mr. Rosen—how he told me, "Some things you won't be able to put in your suitcase; some things are intangible, and yet, you carry them with you."

Now I know what he means.

We eat lunch at Jacob's, a soul food buffet, then Nina and Ava say goodbye and head home. I walk back with Grandpa Earl to his house. When we get inside, I see Dad isn't home yet. I text him: When are you coming home? After spending the day with Grandpa Earl, I am wondering what Harlem treasure Dad will take me to.

Dad writes back, Finishing up my last meeting. I'll be there soon.

Grandpa Earl tells me, "I'll be in here if you need anything," and walks into his sitting room—or at least that's what I call it. There is no TV in there, no phone, nothing but bookshelves against the wall, two armchairs, and a radio on a small table in the corner. Nothing to do in there but sit. Grandpa Earl has the radio on and is leaned back with his eyes closed.

I stand in the doorway, hesitating to bother him, but he said to let him know if I needed something and I need to do this interview. I want to do this interview. I want to learn as much from Grandpa Earl as I can. I can't tell if he's fallen asleep or if he's just resting and listening to the news. I clear my throat, even though I don't really need to. "Grandpa Earl?"

He opens his eyes. "Yes, Amara?"

"I, ah, I was going to ask if I can interview you for my school project."

Grandpa Earl leans over and turns the volume on the radio down. "Well, you really are something. Doing homework on your vacation. I don't know if I've ever met a girl like you." He turns the radio off and says, "Shall we get to it?" He walks over to the living room and sits in an old-fashioned rocking chair. It is dark brown and has a thin pillow in the seat. "Are you recording this?" he asks me.

"Recording?"

"Well, isn't that what a journalist does?" He stands and goes to the cabinet I've been wanting to open. He opens the left door. "You ever seen one of these in real life?" He chuckles. "This used to be your father's tape recorder. He'd walk around the house reciting poems into the microphone and making tapes of his rhymes." Grandpa hands me the tape recorder. "Now, I have no idea if these will even work, but let's give it a try." He pulls out an unopened package of tapes and shows me how to use the tape recorder. "Let's test it out," he says. "We'll need these." He puts in batteries and hands me the recorder.

I hit the Record and Play buttons at the same time like Grandpa Earl showed me.

"Okay, give it a go," he says. "Set it up—introduce yourself and talk about the interview you're about to do."

It feels weird talking into this machine, especially when it's just the two of us. "This is Amara Baker. I am sitting with Grandpa Earl in Harlem, interviewing him for the Suitcase Project."

Grandpa hits the Stop button, rewinds the tape, and pushes Play. My voice booms through the room. It sounds lower than I think my voice normally sounds. Grandpa rewinds the tape again and says, "Okay. This time is the real one. Ready?"

I press the buttons again, and even though I have a list of questions that I wrote down in my notebook, even though I have more questions about Arturo Alfonso Schomburg and Langston Hughes, I don't ask them. Instead, when I open my mouth I ask the question that's been floating in my head ever since our walk from the coffee shop. "Grandpa Earl, what did you mean when you said you didn't understand Dad back when he was a kid?"

Grandpa Earl is quiet for a long time. So long that I wonder if maybe I've upset him with this question, if maybe when he opens his eyes he will tell me to stay in a child's place and stop asking questions that are none of my business. I watch the spokes of the cassette go round and round in the tape recorder. Think how loud this silence will sound when I listen to it later to take notes. Grandpa leans forward, says, "Times were different when I was raising Charles. I think I was trying so hard to teach him how to be a man—a Baker man—that I wasn't always good at letting him be the man he was becoming on his own. Us Baker men are athletes and, well, a lot more rugged than your dad was when he was growing up. I couldn't relate to him. I didn't know how to."

Grandpa stops talking for a moment, then begins again. "You know, one reason why I took you to the Schomburg Center today is because I never took your dad. I wasn't aware of all this when Charles was growing up. It wasn't until after my Grace died that I really understood what she had been saying all along," he tells me. "It was just me in this house. Retired and alone and so I started reading all these books she had around the house, the books your dad had left behind. Made me feel close to her, knowing she had touched the same pages, read the same words. And, well, my eyes opened—I tell you, it was like being reborn. I kind of had to let go of some of my old ways, my ideas of what it meant to be a man."

Grandpa Earl stops talking abruptly and says, "Listen to me. I'm sorry, Amara. This is for your school project.

I don't need to be saying all of this. Do you want to start over?"

"No, no—you're fine. This is, this is exactly what it's supposed to be. My teacher said there's no one way to do it."

Grandpa Earl says, "Well, I guess what I'm saying is, ah, what's that phrase . . . if you know better, do better? Well, I'm trying."

The front door opens. Dad is home, and he has two Nike bags in each hand. I stop the tape recorder and stand up. "Are those for me?" I ask.

"Well, not all of them are for you," Dad says. "I got something for Nina and Ava, too. And my day was fine. Thanks for asking." He laughs.

"Sorry." I hug Dad, and even though I really want to take the bags out of his hands and go through them, I sit back down on the sofa and wait for him to show me what he has.

"What are you two up to?" Dad asks eyeing the cassette player.

"I'm interviewing Grandpa Earl."

Dad sets the bags down and walks over to the coffee table. His eyes focused on the tapes and the cassette player.

"You still have this?" he asks. He picks up the cassette player like it is something precious.

"I have a lot of your stuff," Grandpa Earl says. "I'm sure some of your recordings are stored away somewhere in this house. Your momma made sure of that."

Dad puts the tape recorder down. I think he's going to go upstairs, but instead he sits on the sofa next to me. I think maybe this is a good way to get Dad and Grandpa talking. Maybe I'll have something good to tell Mom when she calls to check in tonight.

I clear my throat. "Grandpa Earl was just telling me how much you loved writing poems when you were in high school."

Dad removes the throw pillow from behind his back, tossing it to the middle of the sofa. He leans back, says, "Was he?"

I look to Grandpa Earl and say, "Weren't you, Grandpa?"

"I sure was, Amara. I couldn't believe how your dad could just make up a poem right out of thin air, not even writing it down." Grandpa Earl doesn't look at Dad when he says this.

Dad says, "But your grandfather wanted me to play ball. Never mind how clumsy I actually was. It was all about the game for him."

I don't know if this is a good thing or a bad thing . . . that Dad and Grandpa Earl are talking about each other, but not to each other.

Grandpa says, "Amara, I have a lot of regrets. A lot of regrets."

Dad gets up, takes the Nike bags, and goes upstairs.

Grandpa Earl watches Dad walk away. He takes a deep breath, looks at me. I don't know if I should continue or stop here, but then he says, "What's your next question?" so I push the Record and Play buttons.

I think of my next question, try to come up with something that will take the sadness out of Grandpa Earl's eyes. "Can we talk about what you're proud of?" I think there has to be something to talk about other than regrets and things Grandpa Earl didn't do so well. He doesn't hesitate to answer. "I'm proud that your grandma Grace and I raised two smart, decent human beings . . . I'm proud of our people, how we've survived what should have destroyed us."

I look at the cassette, make sure it is still turning. I ask Grandpa Earl one of the questions from Mr. Rosen's handout. "What does *your* suitcase carry?"

"Is this suitcase a symbol for my heart, my memories?" Grandpa Earl asks.

I hadn't thought about it this way until he said it. "Yes," I answer. "What does your heart carry with you? What memories do you hold?"

"You know, when I was a young boy my mother took us to the candy store once a week and we'd get caramels and peppermint candies. I would hold on to mine and sit under the porch, savoring it till the candy disappeared from my tongue," Grandpa Earl tells me. "Hmm. I haven't thought about that in a long while, a long while."

I don't ask another question. Just sit and picture Grandpa Earl as a little boy.

He starts up again with another memory. "And, well, I carry the memory of holding my son and daughter for the first time. And of course, I will never let go of your grandma Grace. She shows up from time to time, in my dreams or when I hear a song we both loved."

"I feel her with me, too, sometimes," I confess. "Even

though she had never been to Oregon or to my house I feel her sometimes when I am in the kitchen with Dad and he is teaching me one of her recipes or when I am alone in my room reading a book."

Grandpa Earl smiles at this.

"But being here, in this place, I *really* feel her."

We sit awhile, just being together. No questions, no stories.

I push the Stop button and thank Grandpa Earl for talking with me.

After dinner, once I am in bed, all I can do is think back over everything I saw today. The mural of black legends, the Schomburg Center. I think about my baby sister, how I want to bring her to Harlem one day, how I won't be impatient with her as she takes it all in. How I want to show her where we come from, how I'll whisper in her ear, "You come from greatness, you come from strength."

14

Wednesday starts off the same as yesterday—eating oatmeal and apples with Grandpa Earl. After breakfast, Grandpa Earl leaves to go on his morning walk. Being in this brownstone alone makes me hear every little noise that creeps and creaks. I grab my phone and put on some music so I can drown out the moans of the house, which has a song of its own. I wash the dishes from breakfast, and after, when I walk into the living room, I notice the tape recorder is still on the table. I get to thinking about that cabinet and what else is in there. For some reason, I look around the room before I open the door, even though

I know nobody is here but me. I walk over to the window, look out of it just to make sure Grandpa isn't coming back yet. I tell myself that I'm not being nosy, I'm doing research and that gives me the nerve to go looking through Grandpa's things. I open the cabinet and the first thing I see is a photo album.

I look through the pictures. There's one of Grandpa Earl and Grandma Grace sitting on the stoop. Grandpa Earl's face doesn't have any wrinkles. He looks like Dad. His arms are wrapped around Grandma Grace's waist, and they are caught in a laugh. I look through the rest of the album. There are photos of people I don't know and faces that look familiar. There are pictures of Dad and Aunt Tracey with Grandpa Earl and Grandma Grace. In every shot, Dad is standing next to Grandma Grace.

I want to include some of these photos in my Suitcase Project, but there's no way to make copies of them without asking Grandpa Earl and then he'll wonder how I know about them. So instead, I pull back the thin sticky plastic and take out the photos. They must have been in here forever because it's hard to lift them off the page. I take pictures of them with my phone and just as I am putting the photographs back, I hear keys in the door.

Grandpa Earl is back.

I rush and smooth the plastic back over the photos, toss the album back in the cabinet, and slam the door.

"Hope I wasn't gone too long," Grandpa says.

Uh, no. Nope, you really could've taken your time.

"I stopped at the coffee shop. Brought you back a hot chocolate."

Now I feel bad. "Thanks." I sit in the kitchen at the island and slowly sip. I scroll through the photos I took and realize they're all horrible. They're blurry, and I won't be able to use them.

"What's that frown for?" Grandpa Earl asks.

I put my phone in my pocket. "I, oh, nothing."

Grandpa Earl asks what I want to do today. The truth is all I want to do is spend time with Dad, and since that's clearly not happening, it doesn't really matter what we do. Grandpa Earl says, "You want to take a trip down memory lane?" He walks over to the cabinet and takes out the photo album. The one I just peeked through. When he opens the book, I see a big wrinkle in the plastic cover because I didn't press it down good enough. He looks puzzled and lifts the thin sheet, then slowly presses it down, ironing out the wrinkles with his hand.

We look through the album, me pretending like I haven't seen the photos already, and then I ask Grandpa, "Can we make copies of some of these?"

And it's just that easy. Within minutes we've selected photos and our coats are on and we're heading to the print shop to make copies for my Suitcase Project.

When Dad calls to say he won't be home for dinner, Grandpa orders delivery from a nearby Chinese food restaurant, and we eat dinner while watching back-to-back episodes of *Family Feud*.

Once it's time for bed, we say our good nights and I go upstairs to Aunt Tracey's room. It doesn't take me long to fall asleep, but in the middle of night, I wake up. It is eleven o'clock here, but my body thinks it's only eight in the evening. Back home, I'd be reading a book or talking on the phone to Titus. Here, Grandpa Earl is in bed for the night and Dad is out with Mr. Arnold and a few of his friends from his college days.

The house is quiet. The only noise I hear is from outside: sirens, trucks, a person walking by and talking—

screaming—into their phone. I tiptoe to Dad's room. The headboard has shelves on the side, and I look through the books: *The Fire Next Time* by James Baldwin, *Haiku: This Other World* by Richard Wright.

I think about what Grandpa Earl said, how Dad's old tapes are here somewhere. I want to find them. The first place I look is in the closet across from the bed. I have to stand on a chair to reach the top shelf, which has sealed plastic containers. I take one down, open it. It is full of quilts and blankets. I put it back and take down another. This one has more photo albums and stacks of Polaroid pictures.

There is a second closet in his bedroom, so I go over there. There are no tapes, but there are notebooks. I open the one on the top—it's blue, and the bottom of the cover is loose from the silver rings. Dad's handwriting fills the pages. His poems. I carry the container across the hall to Aunt Tracey's room just in case Dad gets back soon.

I sit on the edge of the bed taking in all of Dad's words. It feels like I'm eavesdropping on a conversation I shouldn't be hearing, like I am finding out his secrets.

I turn through the pages and flip to the back of the

journal. The top of the page says, Things I Want to Do Before I Die. The first thing on the list says, Perform at the Nuyorican Cafe. I don't know if Dad ever did that, but I scroll down his list and see some of the things he has definitely accomplished: Get Married . . . Work at Nike . . . Travel to Japan.

And then the last thing on the list that I'm not even sure he still cares about: Have Dad Listen to My Poetry.

15

"You want to go get some breakfast? I know you've got to be tired of oatmeal." Dad is standing in the doorway, already dressed.

I get out of bed. "And after breakfast what are we going to do?"

"I'm going to walk you over to Tracey's house so you can hang out with Nina and Ava."

"But, Dad, when are we going to spend time together? It's already—"

"Amara, I told you several times—this is a business trip for me."

There's no use in complaining, so I just get ready. As we walk down the sidewalk, Dad says, "You're about to eat the best breakfast sandwich of your life." He zips his coat.

"Better than McDonald's Sausage, Egg, and Cheese McGriddle?" I ask.

"Oh, you have no idea. After you eat this, you will never want McDonald's again."

I doubt that.

We walk to the corner store, and when we get in, I am thinking Dad made a mistake because there is nothing in here but chips and soda, random household items and freezers full of pints of ice cream and Popsicles. A cat strolls by, yawning, and finds a comfortable spot at the back of the store to lie down. "We're ordering food here?" I ask.

Dad walks up to the counter, and even though there's no menu posted anywhere, he orders. "Can I get two sausage, egg, and cheese on a roll?"

"Butter?"

"Light."

"Okay, boss," the man says. He yells the order over to another guy who is standing at an open grill. The cook cracks a few eggs, and they sizzle on the hot iron.

Dad tells me to pick something to drink from the tall coolers lined against the walls. I get a bottle of apple juice and an orange juice for Dad. We eat our sandwiches on the way back to Aunt Tracey's. Dad says, "Told you it would be the best breakfast sandwich you've ever had."

"I didn't say it was the best, Dad."

"Yes, you did. By not saying a word, you've told me all I need to know." He smiles and takes a bite of his breakfast.

He's right. But I don't have to tell him.

We walk three blocks, and then Dad stops in front of an apartment building and says, "We're here."

We walk into the lobby of the building, and Dad hits a buzzer next to a glass door. I hear Ava's voice, "Who's there?"

"It's Uncle Charles and Amara."

"Hello?" Ava yells.

Dad repeats himself.

There is silence, and then a buzzer sounds off. Dad grabs the door quick. We walk to an elevator, and Dad hits the button. We stand for a moment, but nothing dings and the door doesn't open right way. Dad opens the heavy door, says, "Old-school elevators. You've never been on these before, huh?"

"Never," I say, and I feel like I've stepped back in time, but I try not to make a big deal of it because I can just see Ava rolling her eyes at me saying, *What's the big deal, it's just an elevator.*

We get off at the tenth floor.

When we enter Aunt Tracey's apartment, the first thing I notice is how compact everything is. The kitchen can probably only fit two people comfortably at a time, and the dining room really isn't a room but a space in the corner before you enter the living room. But just like Grandpa Earl's house, the walls are covered with photos.

Dad hugs Ava and asks, "Where's your sister?"

"Doing her hair," she says.

"What's today's adventure?" Dad asks.

Ava shrugs. "Haven't decided yet."

I look at Dad. "Are you sure you can't stay? We could all go somewhere together. *Please.*"

"Amara, sweetheart, not today. But—Friday, I'm all yours, birthday girl. We'll do whatever you want, and then in the evening the family will get together for dinner. The

Slam Dunk Contest is on Saturday and the All-Star Game is Sunday. You'll be with me all weekend," Dad says. "And Ava—you, Nina, and your mom are invited, too."

"Thanks, Uncle Charles."

Dad says, "Well, thanks for spending time with Amara." He reaches into his back pocket, pulls out his wallet, and hands me some money "Just in case you need some spending money."

"Thanks."

Dad kisses me on my forehead and leaves.

As soon as he closes the door, Ava says, "Does he always treat you like a baby?"

Nina shouts, "Ava! Leave Amara alone."

"I'm just asking a question. You seem spoiled. What are you going to do when your sister comes?"

"I'm not spoiled," I say.

Just then Nina comes out of her room and I am so relieved. Maybe Ava will stop being so rude now. "Ready?" Nina asks.

I nod. "Where are we going?"

"I was planning on going to the movies and then maybe—"

Ava lets out the biggest, most dramatic sigh. "Do I have to go?"

"Yes, Ava. We're all going."

Ava mumbles, "I don't want to babysit my entire break."

"I'm not a baby," I say.

"Um, yeah, you are. Grandpa Earl and Uncle Charles treat you like you're some fragile piece of china. And you're spoiled—you have it all, don't you? The latest phone, every Nike ever made, designer clothes," Ava says.

Nina tries to say something, but Ava keeps going.

"You're so rich you don't even know how privileged you are. Your dad just throws money at you so you can splurge while you're sightseeing—"

"It's not my fault I have a dad who cares for me," I say. And as soon as I say it, I regret it.

"My dad cares for me. Just because he's in jail doesn't mean he doesn't love me."

"Enough!" Nina yells. "Both of you stop talking. Just stop."

Ava walks away to a room at the end of the hallway, slams the door.

"I'll be right back," Nina says. I hear Nina telling Ava, "You two need to apologize to each other."

Ava says, "I am not apologizing to her. She's a spoiled brat who thinks she's better than us."

I sit in the living room waiting for them to come out. But then I get to thinking, the only way to prove I'm not a baby is to not act like one, and if no one wants to spend time with me or take me around to see the city, that's fine. I'll figure it out myself. I stand up, put my coat back on, and leave.

I'm going to find the Nuyorican Cafe. Going to find out more about my dad.

I look up the directions on my phone and follow the map, which is guiding me to the D train at 125th and St. Nicholas.

Walking down 125th Street all by myself makes me feel powerful. I wish Ava could see me walking and making my way down the block not looking like a tourist or a person who doesn't belong. I walk on the left side of the street. It's still early enough the streets aren't crowded.

Some of the vendors are just now setting up. The man at the corner, the one who sells shea butter and oils, is blasting Bob Marley out of his speakers. The woman behind me sings along until we walk too far and can no longer hear the music.

I walk all the way down 125th until I reach the subway station. I still have the MetroCard Nina bought me, so I don't have to get another one. Once I get to the top of the entrance, I hesitate to go down. This is different from walking around Harlem, this is going underground all by myself. A crowd of people run down the stairs, and a whole nother line of people are walking up. I can't just stand here in the way. I go down.

When I get to the turnstile and swipe my card, the metal bar pushes against my waist. I swipe again. I'm still stuck. A woman in back of me sucks her teeth. "Here," she says, reaching for my card. She swipes it fast and I go through.

"Thank you," I tell her, but she's already halfway down the platform. I see the two signs for the D train. I go to the side where there are less people. I take my phone out and look at the directions again. I count on the map how many stops there will be before I need to get off and transfer for the F train. Three. I need to transfer when the train stops at Rockefeller Center. I do exactly what I did when I was with Nina and Ava—step back away from the edge but not close to the wall. No matter how hard I try not to stare at the tracks where the rats are running around, I can't help it. There's a man leaning against the green pillar in the middle of the platform holding a sign that says, I Ain't Gonna Lie, I Just Want a Beer. He has a cup on the ground next to him. I don't see anyone dropping money in it.

The D comes and I get on. It isn't as crowded as the train was when I was with Nina and Ava. I sit down next to the door and count each time the train stops to make sure I get off at the third stop to transfer.

145th.

155th.

And then the conductor says, "The next stop is 161st Street, Yankee Stadium."

I double-check the directions to make sure I got on the right train. The D. Yes, this is the D.

But it is the D going uptown. I need to go downtown.

I didn't even notice signs for uptown or downtown. I just followed the big orange circle with the letter *D* in the middle.

When the subway stops at Yankee Stadium, I get off.

I don't know what to do. I can't let on that I am lost. Can't look like a stranger who has no idea where they are going. I try to look normal, even though inside I am crying and thinking how Mom always says New York is no place for a girl like me. My hands are sweating, and I am biting the insides of my cheeks to keep from letting these tears fall. I walk over to the man who is working inside the booth.

"Can I help you?" he says.

"Um, yes, I am trying to get to the Nuyorican."

"You gotta speak louder, hon. I can't hear you."

I step closer to the glass window and speak into the tiny holes. "I am trying to get to the Nuyorican."

"The what?"

I pull out the directions again. "Broadway-Lafayette. Does this train go to Broadway-Lafayette?"

"Well, yes. The D goes to Broadway-Lafayette. But you're on the wrong side. You want the downtown train."

He points across the platform at a train whizzing by. "This is the Bronx."

"The Bronx?"

The man steps out from the booth. "Where you from?"

"Harlem," I tell him. He doesn't need to know I'm not from New York.

"All right. Well, you got on the wrong side. Walk up these steps right here, cross the street, and go downtown at the other entrance."

"Thank you."

"You got a ways to go. You know that, right?"

"Yes," I lie. "Thank you."

I walk up the stairs and stand at the corner looking for the right way to go. There's an entrance for the D train on every corner. I see the one that says Downtown & Brooklyn and cross the street. I can't believe I took the wrong train. Ava would definitely be shaking her head at me.

My phone vibrates in my pocket; I take it out. There's a text message from Nina that says, Where are you? Are you going back to Grandpa's? And then another that says, Please call me. She's called three times, and there are five missed calls from Grandpa Earl.

I think, *Maybe I just need to go back. Especially if Grandpa Earl knows.* I put my phone back in my pocket. I'll call them when I get off the subway. I walk down and wait on the platform, checking three times to make sure the sign says Downtown.

I wait.

And wait.

And wait.

No train.

The platform is full, and the man standing near me keeps walking back and forth to the edge and looking down the dark tunnel. "Man, come on. Where is this train?"

I take out my phone. We've been waiting for an hour. I try calling Nina, but I don't have any reception underground. We wait and wait, and finally a train comes but it is so packed no one can get on.

We continue to wait, and the next train that comes is full, but not as crammed as the other one. I get on and hold on to the silver pole in the middle of the car.

155th.

145th.

And then we stop.

At first it doesn't seem like a big deal at all. We're only stopped for a minute. But then the minutes keep passing and passing, and people are starting to get restless. A voice comes on the loudspeaker, saying, "Ladies and gentlemen, we are experiencing delays and will be moving shortly."

More people murmur and sigh and huff and puff.

"Ladies and gentlemen, due to a health emergency on a train ahead of us we are experiencing delays and will be moving shortly."

I feel bad for being so irritated; after all, someone is sick—and on a subway. That must be awful. But I have to get back to Grandpa Earl's before he gets too worried. I only have one stop to go. We wait and wait, and finally, without a voice even coming on to warn us, we start moving again.

When we get to 125th, I forge my way through the crowd and get off. There are so many stairs to climb that by the time I am back out in the cold, I am out of breath and hot. I stand to the side and take my phone out so I can check the time. I touch the Home button and nothing happens; it's still a black screen. I tap it again. Nothing.

My phone is dead.

I don't know why, but of all the things to make me melt into a puddle of tears today, this does it. I know Grandpa Earl probably called my dad, who is probably calling me, and my phone is going straight to voice mail, which is probably making him panic. I walk as fast as I can down 125th to Lenox. I turn left at Lenox and make my way to 129th. It is cold, but I am sweating and sweating. When I turn on my block, I see Aunt Tracey's car parked outside.

Not good.

I walk up the steps and hear Nina screaming, "She's here, she's here!"

Before I make it up the steps, Dad is at the door. "Amara! Are you okay? Baby girl, are you okay?" He grabs me in the tightest hug, and I can feel his throbbing heartbeat. Before I can tell him I am okay he pulls away from me, looks me over, then says, "What in the world were you thinking? You just left? Just up and walked out the house and didn't think to tell anyone where you were going?" Dad is yelling, and there is no more concern in his voice. Just anger. Just disappointment. "I can't believe you, Amara. You know better."

Grandpa comes to the door, says, "Come on, you two, let's bring this inside. Come on now." He ushers us into the house. I take my shoes off and go into the living room, but I don't sit down.

Ava, Nina, and Aunt Tracey are all looking at me, like they expect me to say something, but how can I when Dad is yelling at me.

"What do you have to say for yourself?" he asks.

I don't have anything to say, so I just keep quiet. I have never seen Dad look at me this way. I can't bear to look at him. I turn away, study the grains in the hardwood floor. The last thing I want to do is cry in front of Nina and Ava, and that's exactly what's about to happen if I keep looking at Dad and his I-Am-Very-Disappointed-in-You eyes. "Young lady, you better do some explaining. Where were you?"

For a quick moment, I think maybe I can come up with some story that won't be as bad as the truth is . . . but then I decide on telling the whole truth, because lying might just send Dad over the edge. His face is red, and he looks like he's at that point balloons get to when they have too much air in them. I sit down on the sofa, next to

Grandpa Earl. "I went to the Nuyorican," I tell Dad. "Well, I tried to go to the Nuyorican."

"The what?" Ava asks.

Aunt Tracey gives her a look. Ava sits down on the arm of the sofa.

"What made you think that was a good idea?" Dad asks. "How do you even know what the Nuyorican is?"

"I, well, I found your old poems and journals, and I read through them, and you wrote down that you hoped to perform there one day, so I—"

"Amara, this is unacceptable! You know better than to go snooping through things, and then to up and leave and have everyone worried about you?"

"Well, maybe if you'd spend time with me and actually talk to me, I wouldn't have to snoop around and sneak out."

When I say this, Aunt Tracey stands and tells Nina and Ava to get their coats. "Let's let them sort this out in private," she says. She hurries them to the door, barely giving them enough time to hug Grandpa Earl goodbye. "We'll talk later about these two," Aunt Tracey says to Dad, eyeing me and Ava. Ava won't even look at me.

Once they are gone, Dad doesn't waste time getting back to fussing at me. "You knew I was here for work, Amara—"

"But, Dad, I'm here to learn about you, your childhood, and what it was like growing up in Harlem," I say. "We haven't talked about that at all. You aren't showing me—"

"Amara, you can't put this on that school assignment—no amount of research should have caused you to be so reckless." Dad is pacing around the living room.

"It's not about the homework, Dad. It's about you. I want to know you."

Grandpa Earl says, "Hear her out, Charles. Listen to her—"

"Dad, please stay out of this."

Grandpa Earl walks over to Dad, puts his hand on his shoulder. "Don't be like me, don't push her away." He walks to his room, closes the door.

It takes me a moment to swallow my tears and talk without crying, but finally I say, "I'm sorry, Dad. I was just angry at Ava and—"

"Go to your room. I just—I need a minute." Dad sits on the sofa, his bowed head cupped in his hands.

I walk slowly up the stairs, sit on Aunt Tracey's bed

looking at the walls wondering what they were once covered with. Did she have posters hanging? What happened
to them? What makes a person keep certain things and
throw other things away? I'm in the room for a whole hour
just thinking and thinking. I know I'll be on some kind of
punishment for this. Dad is probably talking on the phone
to Mom right now, the two of them deciding if it should
be losing phone privileges or doing extra chores.

There's a knock on my door. "Amara, it's me," Dad
says.

"Come in."

He opens the door, but he doesn't come in. "Get your
coat, let's go."

16

Dad and I walk on Houston Street and turn left onto Avenue B. "This is the East Village," Dad tells me. "Alphabet City, to be exact."

We turn right on Third Street, and then we walk to a building that has a mural painted on it. One half is of a man's face. His eyes look heavy, like they are holding worry and pain but also passion. "This is Reverend Pedro Pietri. He was a Puerto Rican civil rights activist and cofounder of the Nuyorican." Dad stares at the mural for a moment, and I wonder if his mind has taken him someplace else. "This place is legendary for welcoming playwrights, poets, and musicians of color whose work isn't always accepted by the mainstream industry," he tells me. "That list you saw was something I wrote my senior year of high school. Back when I was a kid, my parents wouldn't let me come down here."

"Why?"

"It just wasn't a place for a kid. At all," Dad says. "Plus your grandpa was not a fan of me being a poet, remember?" Dad touches the mural and begins to walk away. I haven't held his hand since I was little girl, but right now, under the New York sky, I reach out and place my hand in his.

We walk down the narrow blocks, hand in hand. The sky is winter gray, and already it is getting dark even though it's not evening. "Did you ever get to read there?" I ask.

"A bunch of times. When I went to NYU, I was there all the time for the open mic. Your mom and I used to walk this route from our dorm. You want me to show you where I went to college?"

"Yes."

We walk for about twenty minutes, and then we get to a park that has a square white arch at the entrance. "This is Washington Square Park. Our dorm was just a few blocks away," Dad says. "But this was one of our hangout spots. Your mom loved coming here—and Central Park—any green space in the city reminded her of Portland." We sit down on a bench. There are couples holding hands walking through the maze of people. A dark-skinned woman is pushing a stroller and singing to a crying baby. Across from us a photographer is taking pictures, pointing his camera down at the ground and up above his head and every other direction.

"So Grandpa Earl never heard one of your poems?"

"Not for real. Never a formal reading at school and not even if I just tried to read him one at home," Dad says. "My mom did though. She loved poetry, she loved my poems."

When Dad says this he sounds like a little boy, like how I must sound when I brag to Titus whenever Mom or Dad tells me how proud they are of me, how smart I am.

"Writing poems wasn't what Baker boys did. My pops wanted me to play sports, be like him. There were very clear expectations of what I was supposed to be, and it had nothing to do with art, writing, cooking—"

"Girl stuff?"

"Right."

"So he was like Mom?" I say.

"What do you mean?"

"Well, you know, Mom . . . well . . ." I stop talking, but Dad wants to know what I have to say.

"Talk to me, Amara. What do you mean?"

"Sometimes I think Mom wants me to be a *Baker girl*. I think she wishes I was more like her and into girly things."

"Well, I don't know that there are girly things or boy things. You just be who you want to be. We love you for you. It's not based on if you love wearing dresses or not."

"I know Mom loves me. But she's always saying she doesn't know whose child I am, like I don't even belong to this family." I didn't even know how upset I was until I say it out loud. Now I am sitting here like a baby with tears falling down my cheeks.

"Amara, your mom and I love you. She doesn't mean anything by that. She knows whose child you are—you're our daughter, and you have so much of both of us in you."

"Like what?"

"You're smart like your mom. You have her discipline and courage to try new things. You're caring like her, too." Dad kisses me on my forehead. "And from me, well, your mom probably hates to admit it, but you get your fashion sense from me." He smiles, and my tears dry and I sit up straight. "But you're creative like both of us, actually, and I hope you have my compassion and integrity. At least, that's what I try to be in the world," Dad says. "No matter what. You are our everything, and whether you prefer heels or sneakers has nothing to do with our love for you." We sit for a while, and then Dad says, "You know who else you are like?"

"Who?" I ask.

"Your grandma Grace. Sometimes I look at you, and it's like she is standing in front of me. You have her smile, and you're so thoughtful and kind—just like she was." Dad shifts and leans farther back on the bench. "You have all of us in you, Amara. You are all of us." Then Dad says, "You know, you should talk to your mom. Tell her how you feel. I promise you, she has no idea your feelings are hurt. I think she just wants to bond with you, and making clothes for you is her way of showing you how much she loves you.

She isn't trying to make you be someone you're not," he tells me. "You two just need to talk. Something your grandpa Earl and I never did."

"Well, you can talk with him now," I say.

"It's not that simple, Amara."

"You should read something to him. Just pick a poem from your notebook and start reading. Don't you think things are different now? Don't you think he's changed?"

Dad doesn't answer.

I don't say more. I'm not sure it's my place to tell Dad what Grandpa Earl told me, so I just keep quiet and sit with Dad and watch people come and go until he says, "Okay, let's walk by my old dorm and then we'll head back uptown."

We leave the park and walk to the building where Mom and Dad met. Dad's face lights up with a smile as he tells me stories of when they dated. We take the subway back to Harlem, and by the time we come up from underground the evening sky is creeping in.

We walk home, and when we get to Grandpa Earl's block, I ask Dad, "Do you still write poetry?"

"The last poem I wrote was, well, it was for your grandma Grace. I wrote it for her funeral."

Twelve years ago.

"Did you read it at the funeral?"

"No. Your grandpa Earl wouldn't let me. He, ah—refused to put that nonsense, as he called it, on the program. So I didn't go."

"You didn't go to Grandma Grace's funeral?"

Dad shakes his head. "Haven't talked to my dad since, really."

Just before we walk up the steps to the stoop I ask Dad, "What did you do with the poem for Grandma Grace?"

"It's in my wallet, always with me." Dad opens the front door, and we go inside, take off all our layers. Before I go upstairs, Dad says, "Tomorrow the family is going to go to one of my favorite Harlem restaurants, Amy Ruth's. Anything else you want on your birthday?"

This trip to New York has been the best birthday gift ever. Can I really ask for something else? I take a chance, say, "For my birthday I want to hear you read one of your poems."

Mom and I FaceTime like we do every night. When the phone rings, Dad says, "She doesn't know about your solo excursion," and walks out of the room.

And I think Dad not telling Mom about me wandering around New York by myself might be the best birthday gift ever.

I fill Mom in on my time with Dad and tell her about going to Amy Ruth's tomorrow. She talks to Dad for a while, and when he brings me my phone back he says, "Titus called while I was talking to your mom."

I call Titus back. When Titus answers the phone, he jumps right into the conversation. "Are you ever coming back to Beaverton?" he asks.

"I haven't been gone that long," I say. "And the way things were going this morning with my cousins, I kind of wished I was already back home." I tell Titus about my argument with Ava. "I came here to get closer to my family, not argue with them."

Titus laughs. "Every family argues. I fight with my cousins all the time," he says. "Doesn't mean I don't love them. Nobody's family is perfect."

He is so much like his dad, so matter-of-fact and to the point. Titus starts filling me in on everything I am missing. Most of it is pretty boring, predictable stuff except the part about Ms. Sutton being absent for the past two days.

She is never absent. Titus is telling me a very detailed, animated version of how the sub talked and acted and how he doesn't think the sub even knew anything about math. The whole time Titus is talking, I am thinking about what he said about loving family. I am thinking about how love looks so many ways and isn't easily broken.

I am thinking about how even though my grandpa and my dad aren't really talking, they still love each other. I just know they do. I can tell by the way Grandpa Earl says Dad's name, how he stares at him sometimes when he thinks no one is looking. How Dad's eyes change, become warmer, whenever Grandpa Earl says "son."

I am thinking about how Mom shows me her love by making me clothes and massaging coconut oil into my hair. How the bundles of lavender in my closet are a symbol of her care.

I think about Ava and Nina and how even though we are just getting to know each other, there is love there. How Ava looked more scared than she'd admit when they thought I was missing. How Nina just bundled me in, like another little sister.

All the cards and phone calls from Grandpa Earl and Aunt Tracey.

And then there's Big T and Titus buying me shoes, and Aunt Sofie not caring that she is not *real* family, but family just the same.

I have people who love me. I have people to love.

17

Today is Friday, my birthday. When I wake up I think maybe I am not awake, maybe I am still dreaming. There are metallic silver and gold balloons all over the bedroom. The floor is covered. But then Dad opens the door and says, "Happy birthday, Amara," and turns the phone around the room, showing Mom how he decorated the room. I hear her voice saying happy birthday to me, and then Dad turns the phone to face me, so I see her face. It is good to see her brown eyes, her smile. Dad says, "Okay, babe, one, two, three . . ." and they both serenade me with the "Happy Birthday" song. After they sing, Dad hands me the phone.

"I miss you," Mom says.

"I miss you, too. How are you feeling? Is the baby okay?"

"I'm on bed rest, and Sofie is taking good care of me. So tell me, how's your dad? How's Grandpa Earl?" and I know what Mom is really asking.

I tell her, "I'm working on it."

"Well, today's going to be a tough day for them, I'm sure."

Grandma Grace.

"It's tradition for Grandpa Earl and Aunt Tracey to visit the grave site every year. I know your grandma Grace would want your dad there. Make sure he goes. No matter what," Mom says.

"I will," I promise, even though I don't think I can make Dad do anything he doesn't want to do.

After we eat breakfast, Grandpa gets up from the table and says, "Well, I guess I better get dressed. Going to visit my Grace today. Tracey will be here in an hour. You two are coming, right?"

"Yes," I say before Dad can say no. "Dad and I will be ready in time."

When Grandpa Earl goes into his bedroom, Dad says to me, "So you speak for me now?"

"It's my birthday. We're spending it together, doing whatever I want to do. You promised."

Dad gets up from the table, rinses his bowl, and puts it in the dishwasher.

Thirty minutes later, he is back downstairs dressed and ready to go. Nina rings the doorbell, and when I open the door, she says, "My mom didn't want to look for parking, so she had me come get you. She's circling the block."

Grandpa Earl walks behind me, Nina, and Dad. Aunt Tracey's car has two back rows so there are enough seats for all of us. We get into the car—me and Nina all the way in the back, Dad and Ava in front of us, and Grandpa Earl in the front passenger seat next to Aunt Tracey.

I say hello to Ava, and she says hello back, but we both know we need to say more than that. We drive awhile, the whole way singing along to the radio, but then once we exit from the freeway, the car gets quiet. I look out the window; I see tombstones rising out of the ground like flowers, except these stone flowers don't sway in the wind, don't give off a sweet fragrance. Aunt

Tracey parks, and everyone gets out of the car except Dad, so I stay, too.

I am standing on the sidewalk next to the car. His door is halfway open. "Amara, go ahead," Dad says.

"I'll wait for you."

"It's okay. I'm going to stay in the car."

I can't even imagine what I would do if I ever, ever had to say goodbye to Mom or Dad. Just thinking about it makes me dizzy and nauseated and every bad feeling I've ever felt. I stand closer to Dad, as close as I can get, and I take his hand. I don't know what to say, so I just don't say anything and think maybe the words will come. Or maybe it's okay to not always have the words.

We stay like this for a while, and I think about how I've never been to a funeral, but in just one week I have stood on top of someone's ashes and now I am at a grave-yard. I think about how peaceful it felt, how powerful it felt standing on top of the cosmogram at the Schomburg Center. How powerful it felt to take in the spirit of Langston Hughes, honor him. And I think maybe these memorials have nothing to do with the person who left us, but instead are all about the people who stayed. Maybe Mom has it all wrong. Dad shouldn't be here because Grandma Grace would want him to, but because he needs to.

The wind is whispering, chilling the sky with its breath. I try one more time to convince Dad to join everyone else. "Dad, don't do it for anyone else. Do it for you."

Dad gets out of the car, closes the door, and we walk along the path, joining Grandpa Earl, Aunt Tracey, Nina, and Ava. They are all standing there, looking at the headstone, not saying a word. After a long silence, Aunt Tracey says, "I love you, Mom. Miss you every day." Nina and Ava say their I love you's, too. Then Grandpa says a prayer.

They all start to walk away, except Dad.

I stay with him, holding his hand. And then, Dad takes his hand away from mine, goes into his pocket, and pulls out his wallet. He takes out a folded piece of paper that has a thick crease down the middle, unfolds it, and begins to read.

Grandpa Earl, Aunt Tracey, Nina, and Ava stop walking, turn, and listen.

SON TO MOTHER

after "Mother to Son" by Langston Hughes

Momma, you climbed
those splintered stairs
even when there was blood, bruises
from the boards torn up, you kept climbing.

You were light, always.
Sometimes dim, but always
you shined.

Momma, you climbed.
I saw you out of breath, saw you striving
sometimes fast, sometimes slow, but all the time
you kept climbing.

Me, right behind you,
exacting your footsteps
stumbling but never falling,
held up by your faith.

Life for me ain't gonna be the same
without you. But I'll keep on.
And I'll pass you down
to my children, and they will climb too.
They will keep on and on
because of you.

18

Dad wants to make sure we get some daddy-daughter time before dinner tonight, so once we get back to Grandpa Earl's, we leave to explore more of New York. We ride the 4 train into the Bronx. At first we are underground, and then all of a sudden, there is daylight and I see buildings flashing by fast, like someone is shuffling a deck of cards.

"Whoa."

Dad smiles. "Pretty cool, huh?"

"Really cool." I stare out the window, look at the graffiti on the sides of buildings up so high it makes me wonder who could have the nerve to get up there and not get caught.

"So, about yesterday," Dad says.

Here's the punishment. I knew it was coming.

"You need to make things right with Ava," Dad tells me.

"I didn't mean to hurt her feelings. She was being so rude and mean, and I'm tired of her treating me like a baby."

The train stops at Yankee Stadium, but this looks so different from yesterday. I see signs for the D train and realize there are many ways to get to and from a place in New York. It's all so confusing. We walk down the stairs, and once we're outside, I can tell we're not in Harlem anymore. The streets feel more crowded, and instead of brownstones there are majestic buildings that look like old castles taking up half a block. We walk over to Concourse Jamaican Bakery, and on the way Dad says, "The sign of true maturity is when you're able to end the argument first, to forgive a person even if they haven't asked for it. You know, Amara, you keep saying you don't want to be treated like a baby, so you have to stop acting like one."

I know Dad is talking about me and Ava. And I know he's right. "I'll talk to Ava," I tell Dad. "But does this mean you'll talk to Grandpa Earl?"

Dad doesn't say anything.

"Dad, you said forgiving is—"

"I know what I said, Amara."

"So are you going to talk to him?"

"Amara, it's not that simple."

"But it could be. It could be as simple as you telling Grandpa Earl that you love him, that you forgive him. And then, I don't know, just see what happens."

"Like I've said before, you definitely have my persistence."

We get to Morris and 167th, and in the middle of the block, next to a grocery store, Dad opens the door that I barely realized was there. "This is it?" I ask.

"Sometimes less is more," Dad says. We enter the tiny restaurant that doesn't even have tables for you to stay at and eat. It's hard to see who's ordered already and who hasn't, but Dad seems to know. He goes up to the counter and orders two beef patties and two ginger beers. He sees the expression on my face, says, "It's soda. Like a really strong ginger ale."

"Oh." I smile.

Dad laughs.

Dad didn't describe what a beef patty was, so when I see the golden brown pastry, I am surprised. It is stuffed with meat and spices and is officially the best thing I've eaten since being in New York.

We walk around the Bronx, eating our patties and drinking our ginger beers. My soda is too strong, burns my throat. I give it to Dad, who gulps it down in a few swallows. On the way back to the train, Dad says, "Okay, now what's on your list? I'm yours all day."

"All day?"

Dad smiles. "Go easy on me though."

I take out my phone, show him my list in Notes. I know we can't do everything, so I narrow it down: Top of the Rock, Canal Street, Strand Bookstore.

"All right," Dad says. "Let's get to it."

Dad and I head back to Harlem for dinner. "Sorry we didn't make it to all the places you wanted to see."

"It's okay. I saw a lot of places that weren't on the list. Places I didn't even know about."

"We'll have to come back one day. I definitely want to take you to see a Broadway play."

"Promise?"

"Promise."

I really don't know how the day has gone by so fast. I have never walked this much in my entire life. My feet are aching from all the walking Dad and I did. It is already time to meet Grandpa Earl and the rest of the family at Amy Ruth's. We don't even have time to drop our shopping bags off at Grandpa Earl's. When we get to the restaurant, everyone is already seated and waiting for us. Aunt Tracey looks at the bags in our hands and says, "You two are going to need to buy more suitcases to fit all this stuff."

Dad laughs. "She got that shopping gene like Momma."

Nina asks, "What did you get?"

"I bought a few souvenirs but mostly things for my Suitcase Project." I show them the map I got at the Strand, a used picture book that Dad said was his favorite as a kid, and some of the T-shirts I bargained for on Canal Street. "But only this one is for the suitcase," I say, and hold up the I Love NY shirt. "I want you all to sign the heart."

"Oh, I think that's a wonderful idea," Grandpa Earl says.

We open our menus and start figuring out what we want. Every item on the menu is named after a black legend. Dad and I order the Rev. Al Sharpton, which is chicken and waffles. Grandpa Earl gets the Ruby Dee— fried catfish with yams and greens for his sides. Aunt Tracey asks the server for the Gabrielle Union—smothered pork chops. Nina and Ava take forever to decide, and finally Nina gets the Michelle Obama, fried whiting, and Ava asks for the jumbo chicken wings, which is called the Ludacris.

When the food comes, we all swap pieces and share spoonfuls and split the corn bread, and there isn't much conversation. Grandpa Earl says, "Well, this must mean the food is good since no one is talking."

I take this as my cue to say what I need to say to Ava. "Um, I'd like to say something." I take a deep breath and look at Ava. "I want to apologize to you, Ava, and the reason I am doing it in front of everyone is because everyone knows what happened . . . what I said. So, I think they should all hear that I am sorry. And to you, too, Nina. I am really, really sorry for what I said."

No one is eating now. We're all just sitting at the table with a Whitney Houston song blasting from the speakers.

At first I think maybe Ava isn't going to say anything.

Maybe she is not ready to forgive me or talk to me. But after a while, she says, "I'm sorry, too." Then she says, "For everything."

"And I accept your apology," Nina says.

We all start eating again, and we get to talking as if there was never anything that silenced us.

Nina says, "Mom, can we visit Uncle Charles and Amara in Oregon one day?"

And with that question, I start telling them about all the things there are to do, all the places we could go: Multnomah Falls, OMSI, Oaks Amusement Park. And that's just a few. "We could do a day at Seaside Beach. There's all kinds of things to do there, like ride bumper cars, feed the seals—oh, and there's a candy store there that has the best saltwater taffy."

"Okay, okay, slow down," Dad says. "Clearly, Amara will be the tour guide." I hear him whisper to Aunt Tracey, "Leslie and I can cover airfare for the girls."

Grandpa Earl says, "A Baker family gathering next summer. I like the sound of that."

We order dessert, and soon the table is covered with bowls of peach cobbler and plates with slices of sweet potato pie. Aunt Tracey starts telling stories about Dad again. She tells us how in the summertime the fire hydrants would be turned on and they would play in the water, splashing each other and playing tag. And how Grandpa Earl and Grandma Grace took them to see the Christmas tree lighting every year at Rockefeller Center. Then, she tells us stories of Dad breaking her dolls and all the shenanigans they'd get into. "Listen, ladies. There are pros and cons to having a brother." Then she says, "But I admit, we've had more good times than bad."

The stories continue, with Nina and Ava sharing their own tales of sibling shenanigans. We laugh the kind of laughs that make the strangers at other tables look at us, the kind of laugh that burns my eyes and makes my stomach ache. This is the kind of laughter I am having when, through my blurry eyes, I see Grandpa Earl touch Dad's shoulder, and Dad doesn't become a statue or pull away. Instead they look at each other, keep laughing, keep smiling.

We don't want the night to end, but there is a long line of customers waiting to be seated. Aunt Tracey says, "After-party at Dad's?" and we head back to Grandpa Earl's.

Once we're at the house, we sit in the living room listening to more stories about Dad and Aunt Tracey's childhood. Grandpa Earl is sitting next to Dad, and they are going back and forth tag-teaming on a story about the time Dad snuck out of the house and got caught. Both of them laughing so hard they can barely finish the story.

I leave for a moment, go upstairs, and get the tape recorder. I don't want to ask formal questions, just want to get this candid moment of everyone laughing and talking. I push the Record and Play buttons. Capture all this joy.

19

The smell of sizzling bacon, eggs, and pancakes floats through the brownstone. Dad must be cooking. A *real* breakfast. Not oatmeal. I walk into the hallway, and just when I get to the edge of the stairs, I hear Grandpa Earl and Dad talking and so I don't go down. I just sit at the top of the stairs listening to words like "sorry" and "I forgive you" and "I've always loved you" and "I want you in my life," and I think about how much I love words. How mighty powerful they are.

I get ready for the day, putting on my Jordan Retros 1. Today is the Slam Dunk Contest, and Dad is taking me, Nina, and Ava. Aunt Tracey comes, too. When we get to

Barclays Center, Nina and Ava are all big eyed and shocked because they didn't know we'd be sitting in Nike's private suite. "So, wait," Ava says, "we can just get as many snacks and drinks as we want?"

Aunt Tracey says, "Well, yes, but no. Don't overdo it. We're guests here."

Dad says, "You're my guests. You can have as much as you want of whatever you want." We each get a wristband and go inside the room. "Let's get you all your gift bags before we get our seats," Dad says.

Nina opens her bag first. "All of this is for us?" she says. "Thanks, Uncle Charles." She takes out a set of headphones and the newest iPad and holds up the All-Star T-shirt to her body, seeing if it fits. "Thank you," she says again.

Aunt Tracey looks through her bag. "Charles, you are spoiling us. What am I going to do when you leave?"

We all keep digging in the never-ending gift bags. Ava and I go over to the food table and fix our plates. There's all kinds of food on the table, so much that I hope more people are coming because this looks like a lot of food for just the people in this room. Ava and I sit with the rest of the family, who are still not eating.

One of Dad's coworkers comes over and introduces

himself, telling us how much Dad talks about us at work, how he's so honored to finally meet us in person. I know I am smiling so hard right now, but I can't hide feeling good knowing that when Dad travels I am never far from his mind. "All right, so who you rooting for?" the man asks.

Nina and Ava answer, "East Coast," at the same time.

"And you?" he asks me.

"Same," I say.

"Really now?" He shakes his head, pretending to be disappointed. "I gotta go find me some West Coast people." He laughs and walks away, saying, "Enjoy the weekend," as he makes his way to mingle with another family.

Just as the announcer's voice booms through the stadium introducing the start of the game, my phone buzzes. I take it out and see that Hannah is calling. "Hello?"

"Amara, where's your dad? I've been calling him, but he won't pick up." Hannah is talking fast, and there is panic in her voice.

"We're at Barclays Center for the Slam Dunk Contest. He's right here," I tell her. "Hold on." I walk over to Dad, who is taking a picture with some of his coworkers. "Dad, it's Hannah."

As soon as I say that, Dad grabs the phone and walks

184

out into the hallway where it is quieter. I follow him, even though I know he wouldn't want me to. He is too distracted to even notice I am there. He walks halfway down the hall, finds a quiet spot, and leans against the wall. "Is she okay?" he asks. And then so much silence I can barely keep my heart inside my chest. He is nodding and saying, "Uh-huh, okay. Okay," and pacing back and forth. Then he says, "We'll fly out as soon as we can." Dad hangs up the phone, looks at me, and says, "We have to go. The baby is coming."

Saying goodbye is rushed, and I feel like I am forgetting something because I packed so fast and didn't double-check the closet or do one last look-through of the room like Mom always does whenever we travel with Dad and stay in hotels.

Dad carries our suitcases downstairs and loads Aunt Tracey's car. He comes back to give hugs to Nina and Ava, and then he hugs Grandpa Earl. Long, tight.

When they let go of each other, Grandpa Earl looks at me, says, "My sunshine, come here," and he opens his arms wide for me.

I hug him, and he is holding me so tight I think I will feel this hug long after I am out of his embrace.

"Bye, Amara. I'm glad we got to hang out," Nina says. "Can't wait to visit Oregon." She hugs me.

Ava and I say our goodbyes next. After we hug each other, she says, "I hope everything's okay with Aunt Leslie and the baby."

"Thank you," I say.

Aunt Tracey says, "It will be fine. Leslie is at thirty-six weeks. That's not full term, but it's not dire. She'll be okay, she'll be okay." I am not sure if Aunt Tracey believes herself. She repeats it again and again in the car on the way to the airport. "Everything is going to be fine. The baby will be fine. Thirty-six weeks isn't so bad."

These are the only words spoken in the car. Dad is texting and listening to voice mails and texting some more with Hannah. I am sitting in the back seat saying goodbye to New York as it flashes past me. Already I miss this place, but I am anxious to get home. The whole way to the airport I whisper a prayer for Mom, for my baby sister, for all of us.

20

While Dad and I were suspended in the air, flying in the space above the clouds, so close to heaven that our prayers were sure to be heard, Mom gave birth to my baby sister.

Tadala. Tadala means "we have been blessed."

She is five pounds of breath, a tiny girl who cries all night and sleeps all day, who made Dad weep when he first held her in his arms. She likes it when I hold her. I know this because she never fusses when she is in my arms. I am already her favorite, and she's only known me for a few days. Already I love her more than a few days' worth of love.

Today is the first day she is home, and we get to see her without tubes and out of the incubator that looked like a bubble made out of glass with its small hole only big enough to slide your arm in and hold her too-small hand. Now, I can hold all of her. "You can't hold her all day," Mom says. "She's going to be spoiled rotten." Mom takes Tadala from me, but holds her for a little while before putting her in her bassinet. All day, this is what we do—hold her, feed her, change her, hold her, feed her, change her.

This time, when Mom puts Tadala in the bassinet for a nap, Mom goes to sleep, too. Dad tiptoes in the kitchen, fixing a late lunch—which is actually just reheating the feast Titus's mom brought over. She's been bringing food over to the house every few days to help out, even though Mom and Dad insisted that she didn't have to do that. The gray sky has been pouring out rain all day. Dad and I eat lunch together in the kitchen, listening to the noisy raindrops splash and crash onto the windowsill, the pavement. When we are finished, he gets up from the table and says, "Come with me. I want to show you something." He walks upstairs.

I follow him to the attic. It is a spacious room with a low ceiling but big enough for me to stand without having to bend. Dad is hunching, lowering his head. He bends over and pulls the chest that Mom never lets me open into the center of the room.

"Open it," Dad says.

I think maybe this is a trick or something, but he just looks at me until I twist open the lock. Inside the chest there's a quilt made with only black-and-white-patterned fabrics.

"Your grandma Grace made that," Dad tells me. Under the quilt, there is a treasure of journals of different shapes and sizes. Some thick like books, others thin with spiral wire tying the pages together. "These belonged to your grandma," Dad says. "Aunt Tracey sent them to me the year after she died."

Dad picks up one of the journals, the one that is made of black leather with a small gold clasp on the side. "My mom didn't write poetry, but she recorded everything. In the mornings, before the sun was up, she would sit at the dining room table with her ginger tea, writing." He hands me the journal.

I open it and read out loud, let Grandma Grace's words flow through me, let her tell me, in her own words, our story.

21

Our suitcases are due next week. Mom cleared off the dining room table so I could use her workspace. The cherry-wood suitcase sits in the middle of the table. I have the photocopied pictures from Grandpa Earl's album, and I've printed some of the photos from my trip to New York. I even have a few from a walk I took around my neighborhood here in Beaverton. All the images are glued down on the top and bottom of the suitcase, covering the lining. I've stuffed the side pockets with a few of Dad's old tapes, scraps of fabric, and bundles of lavender. I've put some of my poems inside, too.

I've decided to make the bottom of the suitcase look like the cosmogram at the Schomburg Center. My artifact is Dad's tape recorder. I put it in the center, take a blank cassette, and pull all the tape out of it, so it can pour out the open cassette door like a river with many streams. The rivers represented in my display are the Columbia River and the Harlem River. And just like Langston, I'm representing places that are important to me, where I have roots: my grandma's kitchen, my grandpa's sitting room, my school's library, the table in the kitchen where I eat with Mom and Dad, the Schomburg Center, 125th Street, Frederick Douglass Boulevard, Alabama, Louisiana, Oregon. Some of these places I am still getting to know, some of these places I have known all my life. All these places made me, are making me.

MY SUITCASE CARRIES

Grandma's recipes:
a little bit of this, a little bit of that.
Ginger for tea, brown sugar for oatmeal.
A deep pot for stews and soups, an iron skillet
for everything else.
Instructions for stretching a little into a whole lot.

Grandpa's southern drawl,
his slow walk and brown fedora.
A handful of caramel candies and always
peppermint, coffee beans, and cocoa powder.
Old records with jazz moans scratched in the vinyl.

Mom's bundles of lavender for drawers and closets.
Coconut oil for hair, for skin.
Candles to chase away darkness.
How she makes beauty out of every thing she touches.
Her knowing even when no one has told her.

Dad's verbs and nouns,
his tapes and notebooks—
a record of his soul. His voice
always comforting me, telling me I am loved as is.

Gray skies and Oregon rain,
the *beep-beep-beep* of New York streets.
Rivers and roots,
protests and prayers.

All these things
I bring with me.

Author's Note

My personal story is very different from Amara's, but there are some things we have in common. One is our love for Oregon and New York. These two places are home for me, and I enjoyed bringing them together in these pages. Like Amara, I am fascinated with family history, oral stories, and learning about my ancestors. My mother tells me I was her "why child." Always asking questions about the who, what, when, where, and why of a place—of us.

I grew up in a family of storytellers, so answers to my questions were easy to come by. I remember many family gatherings ending with my aunts and uncles reminiscing about what used to be. I loved laughing at the tales my Aunt Mary would share about the shenanigans she got into with my mom and their ten siblings. In every retelling I found myself. I realized who I was more like, where I got my creativity from, whose personality was completely opposite or just like mine. This oral history also taught me about the strength and resilience that was passed down generation to generation, and it made me feel powerful and capable of achieving anything, of overcoming any obstacle I might face. It even taught me how to fail—how to get up after failure and keep going. No family is perfect, and mine has its share of heartbreak and even shame. Knowing this has taught me how to love unconditionally and how to forgive. I have also learned that some family are the people you choose. Like Amara, I have the loving family I was born into, and I also have very special friends who are like family. I am so grateful to have both.

Speaking of my family and friends, I'd like to thank a few: thank you to Jennifer Baker, Ellen Hagan, and Lisa Green for such support while I worked on this book. Our writing dates kept me going. Kori Johnson and Linda Christensen for reading and rereading drafts and offering feedback. And always, thank you to my editor, Sarah Shumway, for your keen editorial eye, patience, and care.

And to my maternal grandparents, to whom this book is dedicated, so much of who I am is because of you. I carry you with me every day.

The Suitcase Project

INTERVIEW QUESTIONS

Interview a special adult in your life. Choose interview
questions from the list below.

- ☐ When you were my age what was something you
  really, really wanted to do?
- ☐ Tell me one story about your mom or dad.
- ☐ What is the name of the city you grew up in?
  Did you like living there?
- ☐ Who was your childhood best friend? What did
  you do together?
- ☐ Do you know the meaning of your name? Do you
  think it accurately describes you?
- ☐ What is something you are proud of?
- ☐ Knowing what you know now, what advice would you
  give to yourself when you were my age?
- ☐ If your life had a soundtrack, name four songs that
  would be on it.
- ☐ What does family mean to you?
- ☐ What do you hope your legacy will be?

WRITING PROMPTS

- [ ] Take a classic poem (like Amara's father did with Langston Hughes's "Mother to Son") and write your own version of it
- [ ] Write a poem listing the people, places, and things in your neighborhood
- [ ] Write a praise poem for a family member or friend
- [ ] Write a poem about a favorite place
- [ ] Write a poem about your family tree
- [ ] Write an apology poem
- [ ] Write a letter to a person who has died. What do you want to ask them? What do you want them to know?
- [ ] Research the year you were born. Find out what entertainment (music, movies, television shows, etc.) was popular, what was happening politically. Write a poem using the facts you learned. Start the poem with the line, "When I came into the world . . ."
- [ ] Write a poem or letter to your future self. What do you want to remember? What do you want to let go of? Who do you want to be?
- [ ] Make a list of the Top 10 Things you are thankful for.

ITEMS TO INCLUDE IN YOUR SUITCASE

- [ ] A photo from your childhood
- [ ] A photo of your family
- [ ] Two inspiring quotes
- [ ] An item that represents the music you love to listen to
- [ ] An item that represents a special place you have traveled to or would like to travel to
- [ ] A menu from a favorite restaurant or a recipe you love
- [ ] A map of a place that is special to you and/or that represents where you are from
- [ ] Lyrics of a song that is meaningful to you
- [ ] An item or image that represents your ancestors
- [ ] Two of your favorite colors

Renée's Personal Top Ten Lists

TOP TEN PLACES TO VISIT IN OREGON:

1. Multnomah Falls
2. Powell's City of Books
3. Portland Japanese Garden
4. Tillamook Creamery
5. Tilikum Crossing: Bridge of the People
6. Saturday Market
7. Bonneville Dam and Fish Hatchery
8. OMSI (Oregon Museum of Science and Industry)
9. Crater Lake
10. Keller Fountain Park

TOP TEN PLACES TO VISIT IN NEW YORK CITY:

1. The Schomburg Center
2. Studio Museum
3. Sugar Hill Children's Museum of Art & Storytelling
4. The High Line
5. Brooklyn Bridge Park
6. Bronx Documentary Center
7. Serengeti Teas and Spices
8. Top of the Rock
9. Riverbank State Park
10. The Langston Hughes House

© NAACP

About the Author

RENÉE WATSON is the multi-award-winning author of many books for children and teens. Renée has worked as a writer in residence for over twenty years, teaching creative writing and theatre in community centres. Along with being a writer, educator and community activist, Renée is the founder of I, Too Arts Collective, a non-profit organisation committed to nurturing underrepresented voices in the creative arts. She grew up in Portland and currently lives in New York City.

www.reneewatson.net

Look out for
more from
RENÉE WATSON
coming soon